W9-BHU-076

WHEN CHAMBRUN CHECKED OUT, MURDER CHECKED IN . . .

Pierre Chambrun, urbane czar of New York's finest hotel, is missing. Laura Kauffman, the stunning swinger whose lovers could fill several volumes of *Who's Who*, has been brutally murdered. And a bomb scare threatens to blow everything sky high.

Who's behind the mayhem and murder? Betsy Ruysdale, the private secretary with a very personal interest in her boss . . . Shirley Thomas, the gossip columnist digging up dirt that could get her buried . . . Claude Duval, the powerful film director who wouldn't take no for an answer . . . Jonathan Harkness, the mysterious Englishman in Penthouse Three? Each of them has a secret . . . and one of them will kill to protect it.

BUT ACCOUNTS ARE ALWAYS SETTLED AT THE BEAUMONT HOTEL.

"Ingenious plotting and wry characterizations."

—*Booklist*

Murder Ink.® Mysteries

DEATH IN THE MORNING—Sheila Radley
THE BRANDENBURG HOTEL—
Pauline Glen Winslow
McGARR AND THE SIENESE CONSPIRACY—
Bartholomew Gill

Scene Of The Crime™ Mysteries

A MEDIUM FOR MURDER—Mignon Warner
DEATH OF A MYSTERY WRITER—Robert Barnard
DEATH AFTER BREAKFAST—Hugh Pentecost

DEATH AFTER BREAKFAST

Hugh Pentecost

A DELL BOOK

Published by
Dell Publishing Co., Inc.
1 Dag Hammarskjold Plaza
New York, New York 10017

Dell ® TM 681510, Dell Publishing Co., Inc.

ISBN: 0-440-11687-2

Reprinted by arrangement with Dodd, Mead & Company

Printed in the United States of America
First Dell printing—October 1980

PART 1

ONE

Pierre Chambrun didn't turn up for breakfast that morning. That was no more unusual than to wake up at nine o'clock some day to find, on looking out the window, that the sun had chosen not to rise.

At precisely nine o'clock on every morning of the thirty years he had been manager of the Beaumont Hotel, Chambrun appeared in his office on the second floor. Waiting for him was the head chef, presiding over a sideboard of chafing dishes and hot plates. You may think that nine o'clock is late breakfast for a busy man, but activities in the hotel rarely allowed Chambrun to hit the sack until after two in the morning. He started the day, each day, with this gourmet breakfast. It ranged from fancy omelets to delicate filets mignons, from salmon steaks flown in from northwestern Canada to one of his special favorites, chicken hash. There was always bacon, cut thick to his special requirement, or a thinly sautéed ham steak. There was toast and sweet butter and wild strawberry jam imported from Devonshire in England. No juice, no fruit, you ask? That came later in the day, on the run, at no specified time. Chambrun did not eat a formal meal again until about nine in the evening.

Chambrun's routines were so exact that any of us on

the staff, confronted with a variation, were instantly
concerned. His failure to appear on this morning was
doubly worrisome because he had done the unusual
by inviting someone to breakfast with him. Normally
he did not speak to me, or to Betsy Ruysdale, his fab-
ulous secretary, or anyone else he may have encountered between the door of his private elevator and the
office until after Jacques Fresney, the current chef,
had presented him with the choices of the morning, he
had savored them and had two cups of American coffee. After that he went to Turkish coffee which Miss
Ruysdale had brewed for him in advance, lit his first
Turkish cigarette, and was prepared to face the world.
To be late for a guest was simply not in character,
certainly not without any message of apology.

Making it more unlikely was the fact that his guest
was a member of the press, a feature writer for *Newsview* magazine. As a rule Chambrun avoids the press
like the plague. He hates anything sensational to be
written about the Beaumont. It is my job, as public
relations man for the hotel, to stand between Chambrun and the average inquiring reporters. But this
was to be special, an article on Chambrun himself as
the legendary manager of the world's top luxury hotel.
Chambrun had agreed to receive Eliot Stevens, the
writer, after persuasions from Frank Devery, the pub-
lisher and editor of *Newsview* and an old friend. A
discourtesy to Stevens was unthinkable.

Stevens had arrived in the outer office on the stroke
of nine. When Chambrun was three minutes late
Ruysdale called his penthouse. Betsy Ruysdale is an
extremely attractive woman in her mid-thirties, fright-
eningly efficient, and rumored to be something more
than a secretary in Chambrun's private life. He neu-

ters her by calling her "Ruysdale," never Betsy—in public.

"I'm sure he's between the penthouse and here," Ruysdale told Eliot Stevens. Chambrun hadn't answered his phone.

"No sweat," Stevens said.

Ruysdale excused herself and went into the private office. Chambrun's office is more like an elegant living room than a place of business. There is a thick Turkish rug on the floor. His desk is carved Florentine, always uncluttered. A Picasso, a blue-period gem, faces the desk from the far wall. It is a place to receive, with charm and elegance, the richest people in the world. They are the Beaumont's guests.

Jacques Fresney was standing by the sideboard, presiding over his silver-covered dishes. He was glancing at his watch. Chambrun was seven minutes late. Fresney asked his question by simply raising his Gallic eyebrows. Ruysdale shrugged and went over to the phone on Chambrun's desk and called me in my office down the hall.

"The Man hasn't shown up for breakfast," she told me, "and Eliot Stevens is waiting for him."

I glanced at my watch. "Eight minutes late. Does that constitute a federal case?"

"Can you remember any time—?"

"No," I said.

"He doesn't answer his phone in the penthouse."

"What do you want me to do?"

"Entertain Mr. Stevens while I do some scouting around."

"On the run," I said.

Eliot Stevens was a pleasant-looking young man, blond, Brooks Brothers dressed. He didn't seem to be disturbed by a ten-minute delay. Ruysdale was cool and outwardly unruffled.

"I'm sure Mr. Chambrun wouldn't want Mr. Stevens kept waiting for his morning coffee," she said, after she'd introduced us. "Do take him in and see that Fresney gives him what he'd like, Mark. I'll see what's holding up the boss."

Stevens and I went through the far door. He was duly impressed by the luxurious elegance of this non-office office. He protested that he was in no hurry for breakfast, but coffee would be nice. We had coffee, sitting in two comfortable armchairs by the windows which looked out onto Central Prak. It was a beautiful day, children playing, equestrians on the bridle paths. All was right with the world, but, you might have said, God was not in his heaven.

"You've worked for Monsieur Chambrun for a long time?" Stevens asked.

"He doesn't like to be addressed as a Frenchman," I said. "He has been an American citizen for the last twenty-five years. He acts and thinks like an American."

"I understood from my boss, Frank Devery, that he was something of a hero in the Resistance in France during World War Two," Stevens said.

"'The black days' he calls them. He was in this country, had just graduated from the Cornell School of Hotel Management when France fell to the Nazis. He went back, did his thing, and came back to take on his job here."

"Took on this job just out of college?"

I nodded. "In those days the Beaumont was owned by George Battles, perhaps the richest man in the world. He lived in southern France. Chambrun saved him from a kidnapping venture by the Nazis. Battles would have given Chambrun his left arm after that. What he did give him was the management of his hotel. He's had it ever since, even though we're now owned by a syndicate of stockholders. The Beaumont without Chambrun would be like—like a Rolls Royce without gasoline."

"He makes it run?"

"With frightening efficiency," I said. "He has a kind of personal radar that somehow keeps him aware of everything that's going on in this place every minute of the day."

Stevens grinned at me. "Then he knows I'm here?"

"Of course he knows," I said.

But Chambrun was now fifteen minutes late.

"I know about the new ownership," Stevens said. "It was George Mayberry—he's chairman of the board, isn't he?—who persuaded Frank Devery to assign me to this job."

"Don't tell Chambrun that," I said. "He and Mayberry, shall I say, don't hit it off. That's putting it mildly. If Chambrun thought he was doing Mayberry a favor, you'd have very slim pickings."

"Thanks for the tip." For the first time Stevens seemed a little uneasy as he twisted in his chair. "What do you suppose is keeping him?"

I wished I had an answer. Nothing less serious than a heart attack or a fall down the elevator shaft from the roof could account for Chambrun's absence. A rudeness was simply not in the cards. If he had been held up by some management emergency he would have phoned Ruysdale with an explanation.

Chef Fresney came over to where we were sitting. "Waiting would be less tedious, gentlemen, if you were to have breakfast. There are filets mignons, chicken hash, mushroom, cheese or tomato and bacon omelets which will take only moments to prepare. This morning there is also Philadelphia scrapple."

"I haven't had chicken hash since I was a kid," Stevens said.

"Ah, then this will bring back your youth, sir," Fresney said. "And you, Mr. Haskell?"

I hated to tell him I'd already had breakfast. I thought I could manage a bacon and tomato omelet.

As Fresney was serving us, Ruysdale came in from the outer office. A tight look around her ordinarily generous mouth told me, without asking, that she had no answers.

"I'm glad to see you decided not to wait for breakfast," she said. "I came in to suggest it."

"No word from him?" Stevens asked.

"I'm sorry, Mr. Stevens," she said. "It's unprecedented, and I can't explain it."

"Perhaps he's ill."

"We've been up to his penthouse. He's not there," Ruysdale said.

"Nice morning for a walk," Stevens said. "Perhaps he lost track of time."

"Mr. Chambrun never loses track of time," Ruysdale said. It was a simple fact. Ask Chambrun what time it is and he would tell you it was fourteen and a half minutes past whatever. Dreaming and losing track of time was not a recreation of his.

Short, stocky, black-haired, and with bright black eyes buried in deep pouches, eyes that could warm with compassion or turn cold as a hanging judge's, Pierre Chambrun is king of an empire that is bounded by the four walls of the Beaumont Hotel. It is like a small city with its own restaurants, bars, shops, a small hospital, an exercise club and squash courts, a heated swimming pool. You can transact your banking business there, make your travel arrangements. It is equipped to handle conventions, fashion shows, balls for charity and for rich little girls' "coming out." There are private dining rooms and private meeting rooms for the boards of directors of big corporations. It has its own police force, presided over by Jerry Dodd, a sharp little man who was almost as sensitive to this private climate as Chambrun himself. I suspect that Ruysdale, Jerry Dodd, and I come closest to knowing Chambrun well of all the large staff. We, by the nature of our jobs, saw it all working at once, whereas many others knew and were responsible only for their own departments. But every one of them knew that Chambrun knew all there was to know about any job, from the lowliest dishwasher to Mr. Cardoza, captain in the Blue Lagoon, the swankest nightclub in the city; from Walters, the Fifth Avenue doorman, to Mr. Atterbury the credit manager; from Mrs. Kniffin, the head housekeeper, to Jacques Fresney, the chef, who drove a Cadillac to work. They all knew the first rule of operating for Chambrun in his hotel: If you don't know the answer to a problem, don't improvise, ask the boss. And they all knew that Chambrun would back them to the limit provided that rule was followed. "If mistakes are to be made, I will make them," Chambrun was known to say. It is only a mild overstatement to say that the people who worked for Chambrun would die for him.

What goes wrong in the Beaumont comes from the outside. It is the home-away-from-home for dozens of United Nations diplomats. People from all corners of

the earth bring their problems, their hates, their political warfare to the Beaumont. There have been murders in the hotel as in any small city. There have been
suicides. Old men die of heart attacks in the beds of
young women they aren't supposed to know. Deals involving millions of dollars are made through our
switchboard. Chambrun presides over this swirling little world, always available, day or night, if there is a
problem. The chief operator on the switchboard always knows where he is. When he leaves his penthouse in the morning he calls Mrs. Veach, the chief
operator on day duty, and tells her he's on his way to
his office. When he arrives there he or Ruysdale lets
Mrs. Veach know he has arrived. He never goes anywhere in the hotel during the day without the switchboard knowing where. The essence of this is that he is
always at the other end of the line for anyone who
needs him.

But not this morning.

He had not notified Mrs. Veach that he was on his
way downstairs. It turned out that the last person who
had talked to him on the phone was Miss Kiley, the
night chief. At quarter past two in the morning he had
made what was a routine call to Miss Kiley. "No more
calls, Miss Kiley, unless there is an emergency." That
was standard, whenever he was ready to sleep. Everyone knew that he was not to be interrupted after that
except for an emergency, and if an emergency was
claimed and it turned out it could have waited till
morning the boom was likely to be painfully lowered.
Miss Kiley wouldn't have connected anyone from the
outside, except perhaps the President of the United
States—and he would have to give a reason.

No one had called from inside or outside the hotel.

No one had heard from Chambrun after that good-night shutoff. He wasn't in his penthouse. So far no one had been able to locate him anywhere else in the hotel. It was the first time in all my years at the Beaumont that I had no way to locate him.

As I watched Mr. Stevens enjoy his chicken hash I could feel a lump, like a hard fist, forming in my gut. I was suddenly scared. Chambrun was now forty-five minutes late.

Ruysdale reappeared. She entered behind Stevens and gave me a little negative shake of her head. Nothing—or, it turned out, nothing that did anything but increase anxiety.

"Mr. Stevens, I'm dreadfully sorry," Ruysdale said, "but I just don't know what can have happened to delay Mr. Chambrun. I know when he does come he will have an explanation and a humble apology for you."

"Tell him all is forgiven if he'll invite me to breakfast again and have chicken hash. My God, that was wonderful," Stevens said.

I don't think he was aware of the tensions around him. He went off cheerfully after giving Ruysdale a private number where he could be reached. He didn't seem to notice the little man standing by the windows in Ruysdale's office.

It was Jerry Dodd, our security officer. The minute he was alone with Ruysdale and me, he turned from the windows. I don't think I had ever seen him so tense. Tense and coldly angry.

"Mrs. Kniffin has just reported," he said. Mrs. Kniffin is the hotel's head housekeeper. "It's routine for maid service to go into the boss's penthouse about ten o'clock in the evening, turn down his bed, and put out clean pajamas for him. That's if he isn't there. They

went in last night, did their job. Mrs. K. reports now
that his bed was never slept in, pajamas not used."

"But he called Miss Kiley on the switchboard at two
fifteen?" Ruysdale asked.

"So whatever happened, happened after that," Jerry
said.

"What happened? What do you mean 'whatever
happened'?" I asked.

"I don't know what I mean," Jerry said. "You got
any bright ideas, Mark?"

"First time in the ten years I've known him he
hasn't followed routine."

"Hell, man, I know that!" Jerry said, as if he hated
me for reminding him.

"So what explanation can there be?" Ruysdale
asked, still cool, still outwardly unmoved. But I knew
her heart must have felt cold behind her handsome
bosom. She loved the man, whether or not there was a
special physical intimacy between them.

"A man in his fifties," Jerry said, "working round
the clock at high pressures, could be subject to a heart
attack. But he has to have it *somewhere!* I've alerted
every place from the roof to the subcellars. Nothing.
There are, of course, eight hundred and twenty
rooms, all occupied by someone. And there are
hundreds of offices, closets, storage places to be
checked."

Ruysdale's tapering fingers gripped the edge of her
desk. "You have to begin at the beginning, Jerry," she
said. "He didn't check with the switchboard when he
left his penthouse. First time ever. Why? He didn't
have a heart attack or an accident in the penthouse or
you would have found him there."

"We have to go back to two fifteen A.M.," Jerry said.

"He was okay then. He called Kiley in the usual fashion."

"We don't know he was all right then," Ruysdale said. "If someone was with him. If he—if—"

"You're suggesting—?"

Ruysdale looked at Jerry and then me. Fear had darkened her eyes. "He wouldn't leave the hotel voluntarily without checking with the switchboard. He wouldn't voluntarily change his routines without explaining in advance."

"You keep saying 'voluntarily,'" I said, knowing damn well what she meant. Only a crippling health seizure or a violence could account for his behavior. Since a preliminary search had failed ot locate him, the health theory was doubtful. Violence, then. What kind of violence?

Jerry Dodd was thinking right along with me. "Let's take the grimmest possible view of it," he said. "Somebody out to get him."

"Why?" Ruysdale asked.

"Never mind 'why' for the moment," Jerry said. "Let's suppose someone was holding a gun on him when he checked out with Miss Kiley at two fifteen this morning. There would then be no calls, no interference. So, some maniac kills him."

"No!" It was a whisper from Ruysdale. Her lovely face had turned a sort of chalk white.

"So where is the body?" Jerry said, cold, matter-of-fact. "There are places it could be hidden—closets, storerooms, hundreds of rooms occupied, one possibly by some psychotic freak. If there is a body, it has to be somewhere in the hotel. We'll find it, sooner or later."

"How much sooner?" I asked.

"Mr. Chambrun and I figured it out once," Jerry

said. "Take six crews of two men each, ten minutes to each room. It would take a day and a half, thirty-six hours, to cover every place and come up empty."

"Oh, God!" Ruysdale said.

"There's no way for anyone to lug a corpse out of this hotel without being spotted," Jerry said. "Even if it was stuffed into a trash barrel, it would be found in the subbasement where trash is checked over before it's carted away. Chambrun himself would know how to get out of the hotel without being spotted because he knows where every check spot is and how security is rotated."

"With a gun at his back?" I asked.

"If he thought his best chance lay that way," Jerry said.

"A kidnapping?" I suggested.

"If that's it we can expect some kind of demands from someone presently," Jerry said.

Betsy Ruysdale drew a deep, shuddering breath and then straightened up in her chair. Dear Miss Efficiency! "I can see the boss walking in that door sometime from now and demanding to know what the hell is the matter with us," she said. "There is a hotel to be run. You and I are going to have to do it, Mark, while Jerry keeps searching." She glanced at a calendar on her desk. "He has an appointment with George Mayberry at eleven o'clock. Meanwhile there is a whole schedule of events for the day, Mark. That's your job."

I nodded. There was, I knew, a fashion show starting fifteen minutes from now. Also a convention of governors from the northern states, an all-day hassle. There was a benefit ball for the Cancer Fund in the evening, a big society-type wingding. In the early hours of tomorrow morning the lobby and the Tra-

peze Bar were to be turned over to a film company
for shooting footage for some super-spectacular di-
rected by Claude Duval, the famous French genius.
This filming had been foisted on Chambrun by his
board of directors and over his dead body, God forgive the phrase. It was my business to see that everything was properly prepared for these happenings,
properly executed when they began.

Yes, there was a hotel to run, and the best thing we
could do for a missing Chambrun was to see that
nothing interfered with his Swiss-watch perfection of
performance.

It is difficult to describe the atmosphere in the
Beaumont that morning to someone who doesn't understand the workings of the staff, what Chambrun
calls his "family." Outwardly the hotel went its cool,
smooth way. Guests smiled at staff, unaware of any
problem, and staff smiled at guests, hiding an anxiety
that had spread in their ranks like a plague.

The first item in the daily routine that was ruptured
by Chambrun's absence was the morning examination
of registration cards. They were on Chambrun's desk
ready for his attention when he got to his first cigarette of the day along with his first cup of Turkish
coffee. Guests of the Beaumont might have been a
little disturbed by how much information the management had about them. When they registered, several
people made a notation on the card before it reached
Chambrun. Credit ratings were supplied by Mr. Atterbury, ranging from unlimited down through A, B,
and C. The cost of a stay at the Beaumont was no
laughing matter. Security supplied other information.
A for an alcoholic, WC for a woman chaser, XX for a

man double-crossing his wife, WXX for a woman
double-crossing her husband, G for gay. After Chambrun had looked at the cards, you might find his initials, P.C., in a bottom corner, which meant that
Chambrun had special information about the guest
which wasn't for general consumption.

I looked at those cards, which lay neglected on
Chambrun's desk. Part of my job was to pay special
attention to guests who rated it. The movie people
were the most interesting. They had checked in the
night before. They all had unlimited credit. Two
items were on the fascinating side. Janet Parker, the
girl star, had nothing but a credit okay after her name.
Robert Randle, the glamorous male star, rated a G.
What would his army of women fans think if they
knew it? Hell, it was probably no secret in the film
world, where people were probably laughing up their
sleeves at the rumors in the gossip columns that Bob
Randle and Janet Parker were "like that." Security had
nothing on Clark Herman, the producer, except a B
for bachelor. Claude Duval, the maestro, the French
director, had even less, except a note from Jerry Dodd
saying he wanted no interviews, no photographs, no
special publicity. "A loner," Jerry had written, "with a
phobia about privacy."

There was only about eight other cards, all people
who had histories as guests of the hotel. Most of the
Beaumont's guests are repeaters. Of course Chambrun's initials appeared on none of the cards because
he hadn't seen them.

I made a mental note of the fact that flowers should
be sent to Janet Parker's suite in addition to the usual
fresh fruit and champagne that went to every guest
when they registered. I went down to the lobby.

There the climate of strain was obvious to an insider.

Johnny Thacker, the day bell captain, was helping a newly registered guest to the elevators with his luggage. I recognized a late-arriving governor for the politico's convention. Johnny had on his best smile for an important guest, but when he turned to me the smile vanished.

"Anything?" he asked.

I shook my head.

"Jesus!" Johnny said, and went back to his governor.

Mr. Atterbury, the credit manager, gave me an imperceptible signal from the front desk.

"News?" he asked, when I joined him.

"Nothing," I said.

Atterbury gave me a feeble smile. "Maybe no news is good news," he said.

"Let us pray," I said.

The governors were beginning to gather in a small ballroom off the lobby and I went there. At the door I ran into Ralph Crowder, their press representative and an old acquaintance.

"We'd hoped Chambrun would be here as we begin," he said. "He's always had a little speech of welcome for the governors, and he does it so well."

"Unfortunately, Mr. Chambrun is involved with an emergency," I said.

"I didn't know there were ever emergencies at the Beaumont," Crowder said.

I tried a smile. "A leaking faucet is an emergency to Mr. Chambrun," I said. "That's why the Beaumont is the Beaumont."

"That's good," Crowder said. "May I quote you when I explain his absence?"

"When you explain his absence I'll buy you a steak

dinner, which costs about twenty-five bucks in this joint," I said.

That went over his head.

"Anything out of order? Anything you need?" I asked.

"Everything is perfection as usual," Crowder said. "When Chambrun gets a new washer in his faucet tell him we'd still like to see him. Perhaps he'd drop in at the lunch break."

"I'll make a note of it," I said.

I called my office on the second floor. My secretary had a message for me. "When you can. Shirley." That was the message.

Perhaps I should take time out to repeat something I have said before. About every four months I fall in love forever. It used to be every six months. I was in love forever on that morning when Chambrun failed to appear. Her name was Shirley. Shirley Who? That isn't a question; it's the way her syndicated gossip column is signed. "Shirley Who?" In the beginning, when she started writing the column, the idea was to hide the identity of this female Peeping Tom. But after about five years of lifting the lid on the juiciest scandals from coast to coast it became generally known that Shirley Who was really a strikingly beautiful blonde named Shirley Thomas. A Peeping Thomas, I called her.

My in-love-forever situation of the moment was approaching the rocks the day I met Shirley. I don't think her interest in me amounted to much more than that I, Mark Haskell, public relations man for the Beaumont, might be a source of items for her column. I don't think the fact that we wound up making love

Death After Breakfast   23

that first day I met her was any sort of a bribe on her part. She enjoyed sex with any sort of male man. She was something very special, I don't mind saying.

I think I should deliver a short lecture at this point. Attitudes toward sex in this day and age bear no resemblence to the attitudes of my father and mother or yours. Romance is almost a forgotten ingredient. Sex is an activity, a sport. Sex magazines are all over the newsstands, revealing all there is to reveal to both men and women. Nice girls out of finishing schools talk about it in the four-letter words of the barnyard. Men have always played the field. Now women play the field without any damage to their reputations or standing.

I was glad of that change of attitude that first evening with Shirley. She came to my apartment on the second floor of the Beaumont. I didn't have to show her any etchings. We both knew what we wanted and why she was there.

I remember it was a Friday night because of what followed. About midnight, after a marvelous passage together, she kissed my cheek and sighed and said she had to go home.

"I need to get some rest and freshen up for tomorrow," she said. "I'm spending the weekend on Tex Holloway's yacht. He's the Texas oil man, you know."

I didn't know, and I was surprised to feel a sharp stab of jealousy. I had no right to, but I felt it.

"How is sex on a yacht?" I asked her.

She gave me a dazzling smile. "Rather unusual," she said, "specially if the seas are running high. Added motion you wouldn't believe."

So I lay there in bed watching her dress. I felt a

kind of schoolboyish anger when she kissed me on the
forehead and left. She had no right to walk out on me.
But of course she had every right.

The next morning, a few minutes before nine and
my daily appointment with Chambrun, my phone
rang as I was coming out of the shower. It was Shirley.

"Not on the oil man's yacht yet?" I asked, acid drip-
ping.

"I'm not going, Mark."

"Oh?"

"I have the feeling it matters to you," she said. "If it
does, I discover I don't want that."

I could have told her not to be a damn fool and that
would have been that, but I felt an unexpected surge
of relief.

"That's the greatest speech since the Gettysburg
Address," I said.

"Lunch?" she asked, and I thought she sounded re-
lieved.

"Lunch, dinner and breakfast," I said. And then I
added what may have been a fatal word. "Forever," I
said.

"You're a love, Mark. One o'clock?"

That's how it began. And now, after three months,
it had become apparent to me that Shirley was not so
cynical about romance as she had made me believe.
This could be forever, I told myself.

So that fills you in on Shirley Who? Her message
simply meant she wanted me to call. Much as I loved
her—at the moment—it was not an ideal time.

She sounded bright and businesslike, probably
working on her column.

"How are you this morning, darling?" she asked.

"A little harried," I said. "Lots of goings-on." Even Shirley couldn't be told about Chambrun. I would trust her with my life but not with a secret.

"Claude Duval is starting his filming there tonight, isn't he?" she asked.

"They're taking shots at the Cancer Fund Ball," I said, "and then, when the bars are legally closed, the actors will go to work with scenes shot in the lobby and the Trapeze Bar."

"I'll be at the ball, of course," she said. "But I wondered if, when Duval goes to work, you could hide me away in the woodwork somewhere. I'd like to see him work."

I laughed. "The price will be high," I said.

"Of course, luv, and I promise to pay and pay and pay."

"Breakfast?" I asked.

"Naturally," she said.

The mills of the gods were grinding, but I didn't know it at the time.

Chambrun was nearly an hour and a half missing, and George Mayberry was fuming up in Ruysdale's office. Chambrun was not late for an appointment with the chairman of the board.

I have a simple four-letter Anglo-Saxon word to describe George Mayberry which I can't use here. He is a big man—physically. He has a loud voice and he scowls a lot, self-importantly. He dresses expensively but conservatively. He demands and expects instant service at the snap of his heavy fingers. He meant to look and sound formidable, but I had the feeling that if you stuck a pin in him he would deflate like a pricked balloon, dissolve like the Wicked Witch of the East in *The Wizard of Oz.*

Mayberry was a sort of one-man oversight committee for the board of directors. It is ironic, because he knows as much about the management of a hotel as I do about the construction of a nuclear submarine. I am of the opinion that wiser heads on the board had given this big windbag the job to get rid of him, convinced that Chambrun could make chopped liver out of him.

Unfortunately, that morning Chambrun wasn't there to do the job. Mayberry was steaming at Ruysdale. I suppose he thought he was confronting a "helpless woman," the perfect target for his bullying tactics. He didn't know he had a tiger by the tail.

"He's late for an appointment with me," Mayberry was thundering as I walked into Ruysdale's office.

"I regret to say he didn't show up at all for an earlier appointment," Ruysdale told him.

"Where is he?"

"I'm afraid I don't know, Mr. Mayberry."

"Don't know! Aren't you his secretary! Doesn't he keep you informed as to where he is on a business day?"

"Ordinarily."

"So what the hell is this?"

"An unusual circumstance," Ruysdale said quietly.

The phone on her desk rang and she picked it up, moving very quickly. "Miss Ruysdale speaking." Then: "Yes, Jerry. . . . Oh, my God! . . . Yes, of course you must. . . . I'll tell Mark."

She looked at me as she put down the phone, the color drained from her face. I didn't want to hear what she had to say. Bad news about Chambrun, I was certain.

"There is a problem in Suite Twenty-one A," she said.

"What kind of problem?" Mayberry wanted to know.

"Jerry Dodd thinks it's a homicide."

"Who is Jerry Dodd?"

The oversight chairman didn't even know the name of the hotel's security officer. Ruysdale didn't answer his question.

"Laura Kauffman," she said. "Mrs. James Kauffman. Big wheel in the social world. The former Baroness von Holtzmann. Chairperson of the committee that's running the Cancer Fund Ball tonight."

"My God," Mayberry said. "I know Laura Kauffman well!"

"Jerry has called Homicide," Ruysdale said. "You'd better get up there, Mark. We've got to keep the press away in case the facts have leaked, at least until—"

Until, or if, Chambrun put in an appearance.

I headed for the door.

"I'll take charge here," I heard Mayberry say.

I didn't pay any attention to him.

TWO

Anything Jerry Dodd did he did thoroughly. His search for Chambrun was slow and methodical, but none of the ground would have to be covered again. Part of the process begun that morning was sending teams of two men to every guest room in the hotel. They announced themselves as maintenance men if the guest was in. Some kind of electrical emergency that couldn't wait. The possibility of a short circuit that might in turn start a fire. Irritated or not the guests let the "maintenance men" look. Where no one answered a doorbell ring the searchers used a passkey to get in. That was how Laura Kauffman was found in Suite Twenty-one A. No answer to the doorbell and the searchers had let themselves in.

When I arrived on the twenty-first floor I found one of Jerry's men standing outside the door, a man named Sims.

"I was told to let you in, Mr. Haskell," Sims said. He had a key.

"Thanks," I said.

"I hope you've got your stomach screwed in tight," Sims said. "It's not pretty."

Sims opened the door and I went in. Twenty-one A is a typical small suite: a foyer, a living room, a bedroom, bath, and kitchenette. Suites in the Beaumont are decorated in different styles, from Louis the Fourteenth to frightening modern. Twenty-one A is early American, with a Grant Wood and a Benton decorating the panelled walls.

Jerry Dodd turned from the windows as I came in. He nodded toward the bedroom door. "Keeping it shut till Hardy gets here," he said. "Thank God I was able to get to him."

Lieutenant Hardy of Homicide is an old friend who has been involved with Chambrun during other violences in the past. He is a big blond man who looks more like a not quite bright Notre Dame fullback than a very shrewd detective.

"What happened?" I asked.

"A bloody horror," Jerry said. A nerve twitched high up on his cheek. "Maybe twenty stab wounds. Her breasts, her stomach, other unmentionable areas. My guess is that the Medical Examiner will tell us it was a rape and a murder."

"My God!"

"What do you know about Laura Kauffman, Mark?"

"Nothing, really," I said. "Ruysdale just said she is— was—a big wheel in the social whirl. Used to be the Baroness something-or-other. She was chairman of the Cancer Fund Ball tonight."

"Your girl friend," Jerry said. "She should have a rundown on her. See what you can dig up. Hardy's got to have some place to start."

As I was starting for the phone the outside door opened and Sims stuck his head in.

"A Mr. Mayberry insists on seeing you, Jerry. He says he's in charge."

Mayberry didn't wait for an answer. He shoved Sims aside and came barging into the sitting room.

"Now what's going on here, Dodd?" he asked.

Jerry, who was half Mayberry's size, gave the board chairman a fishy look. "Out!" he said.

"Now just who the hell do you think you are?" Mayberry shouted.

"Oh, I know who I am," Jerry said. "Just who the hell do you think you are?"

Mayberry looked close to apoplexy. "Tell him!" he said to me.

"Mr. Mayberry is chairman of the board of directors of the owners' syndicate," I said.

"Well, bully for him," Jerry said. "The message is still 'out.'"

"I'm a good friend of Mrs. Kauffman's," Mayberry said. "I demand to know—"

"Out!" Jerry said. It was the whisper of a snake about to strike.

"I'll have your hide for this, Dodd!" Mayberry thundered.

"Sims!" Jerry said.

Sims had been pushed aside by Mayberry, but that was because he wasn't expecting anything. He made a swift move up behind the big man, caught his arm and twisted it sharply behind his back. Mayberry made a sound that was almost a scream.

"Do what the man says," Sims said, sounding very polite.

Mayberry was forced out of the room and into the hall, shouting that he would fire everybody on the staff if necessary. The closed door shut the noise of him out of the soundproof suite.

"If we find Chambrun, nobody will be fired," I said.

"If we don't find him, it won't matter," Jerry said. "Try to get onto your girl, will you?"

I called Shirley. She sounded surprised to hear from me so soon again. "You decided to buy someone else lunch," she said

"Never," I said. "But I've got trouble you can help me with."

"Name it."

"What do you know about Laura Kauffman?"

Shirley laughed. "More than would make her happy to know that I know."

"Could you come over here with what you have?"

"Oh, Mark, I'm trying to finish a column before our lunch date. Won't it wait?"

"It won't wait," I said.

"Why not?"

"Somebody has been caught dead here," I said. "It's important for us to have a dossier on Laura K."

"She killed her husband!" Shirley said.

"You want a scoop, you'll have to come over here to get it," I said.

"Give me a hint."

"I don't trust the phone," I said.

"Yours or mine?"

"Mine. It goes through a switchboard. Lather up the horses, will you, luv?"

"Mark, if this is a game—"

"I've never been more serious in my whole life," I said.

The burly figure of Lieutenant Hardy appeared in the doorway, followed by his crew of homicide specialists, photographers, fingerprint men. His first question was not unexpected.

"Where is Chambrun?" he asked. When there was big trouble Chambrun was always on hand.

Jerry told him where Chambrun wasn't. They had found what was in the next room while searching for him.

"Want me to put out an APB on him?" Hardy asked.

Jerry looked suddenly very tired. Dealing with a murder served only to sharpen his investigative wits, but searching for Chambrun, a man he loved, produced an anxiety that had worn him down.

"I'd be glad of any help," he said. "Searching the hotel is a routine I can carry out, but every instinct I have tells me we're not going to find him in the hotel."

"Kidnapping?" Hardy suggested.

"Maybe. But nobody's made any demands yet."

Hardy went to the phone and ordered an all points bulletin set in motion at police headquarters. Then he and Jerry went into the bedroom where Laura Kauffman had been brutalized. I could have gone with them but I didn't want to see what was there. Jerry's description had convinced me my stomach wasn't screwed in tightly enough.

I called Ruysdale on the phone and told her Hardy had arrived. On her end she'd heard nothing, but she reminded me of a fact that was hard to keep in focus. There was a hotel to run.

"Claire DeLune has been screaming her head off for Chambrun or you. Things are not the way she wants them in the small ballroom. I guess you're elected, Mark."

"Oh, God, Betsy," I said. "I don't give a damn about fashion shows at the moment."

"You're still working for Chambrun," Ruysdale said very quietly. "He'd want everything covered, Mark."

"I know," I said. "So mine 'not to reason why—' "

Claire DeLune was the name a Brooklyn-born girl named Gussie Winterbottom had taken when she entered the field of fashion design. She was a hard-driving, very efficient and talented woman. At forty she could almost have passed for one of her own very beautiful and talented models, except that she had replaced youth with a kind of lacquered finish. She dressed in her own designs and they were pretty sensational.

"Hi, Gussie," I said, when I found her in the small ballroom.

"Keep you scurrilous tongue off me, you bastard," she said. She didn't like to be reminded of her real name. "Where is Chambrun?"

"Tied up," I said, and almost choked when I said it.

"I was promised mirrors," Gussie said. "Six full-length mirrors in the dressing room. How do you expect my girls to get put together if they can't see what they're doing?"

"Six full-length mirrors," I said, trying to concentrate on where they could be found.

"So get off your butt and produce them," Gussie said. Her eyes narrowed. "There's a rumor around that Chambrun has skipped town."

The news was beginning to leak. Too many people were involved in the anxious search.

"Your models drive him up the wall," I said. "They remind him of his youth."

"Don't *you* get any ideas about them, buster," Gus-

sie said. "They're not here to titilate the male popula-
tion. They're here to sell dresses to women. Six full-
length mirrors on the double, please. That 'please' is a
figure of speech!"

A half-naked girl appeared in the doorway to the
dressing room. "Madame DeLune, if you could—"

I might as well have been wallpaper as far as the
nude model was concerned.

"You see, she needs a mirror!" Gussie said, and
charged off.

In the lobby I got in touch with the supply department and asked for six full-length mirrors on the double. "Her show begins in less than an hour."

"I'll have to steal a few somewhere," the supply department told me.

"There's one on the back of my bathroom door," I
said.

As I put down the house phone I saw Shirley
coming toward me across the lobby from the front entrance. She was carrying a briefcase under her arm.

I'm not much at rhapsodizing in words. I have
thought of other women "forever," and at the time I
thought that, was convinced that each of them was the
most beautiful ever. But, whatever my bias at the moment, Shirley was the most. Her blond hair, worn loose
and down to her shoulders, was really gold. She was
small-boned and she moved with the grace of a ballet
dancer. Her wide blue eyes were devoid of any sus-
picion or cynicism. Beauty, I think, is as much per-
sonality as bone structure, skin texture, or measurements. The girl was so open, so apparently uncom-
plicated, so genuine that she took your breath away in
a world of neurotics and psychos, in a world where a
Chambrun could be whisked away into oblivion and a

woman could be butchered in her bedroom in a civilized hotel. I wanted to take her in my arms as she came up to me, but I restrained myself. Too many people had their eyes on her as she crossed the lobby. I took her by the arm, without speaking, and led her toward a small private office back of the main desk. I guess, when she looked at me, she saw that the situation was real and serious.

In the small office I kissed her.

"Just seeing you lifts loads," I said.

"Mark, what is it?"

I sat down beside her on a green leather sofa and took her hand. My hand wasn't steady.

"Whatever I tell you is strictly off the record," I said. "Don't protest, luv. When I tell you, you'll see why." She waited, without comment. "Chambrun has disappeared. We suspect some kind of violence, perhaps a kidnapping."

"Mark!"

"In searching for him we have been going from room to room in the hotel. We didn't find him in Laura Kauffman's suite, but we found her. She had been assaulted, probably raped, and stabbed about twenty times."

"My God!" Her hand tightened in mine.

"The police need whatever they can find out about Laura. That's why I asked you to bring what you have."

"But, Mark, what I have is just—gossip!"

"Probably truer than the truth," I said. "You ready to go up to talk with Hardy? He's the homicide man."

"Do I have to see—?"

"No, luv."

We went up to twenty-one and found Sims back at his post outside the door of Suite A.

"What happened with Mayberry?" I asked him.

"First he is going to complain to the mayor, and after that the White House," Sims said.

He took us into the suite. The living room was deserted. Sims knocked on the bedroom door and asked for Hardy. The big detective came out of the murder scene after a moment or two.

He acknowledged my introduction to Shirley with a pleasant smile. She made people smile, even in a situation like this. "I read your column each day it appears, Miss Thomas," he said. "Sorry to drag you into this mess."

"I don't know how I can help," she said. "She has a husband, you know, James Kauffman. They've been separated for some time, but he should know a great deal more about her than I do."

"Among the missing so far," Hardy said. He gestured Shirley to a chair.

She started to open her briefcase. "The thing that seems unlikely, from what Mark told me, is rape."

"Oh?"

"Rumor has it that she will say yes to anyone, from the grocer's delivery boy and the milkman to a complete stranger on the street corner. She wouldn't have put up a fight to avoid sexual acrobatics with anyone."

"The woods are full of psychos, Miss Thomas," Hardy said. "This one probably didn't stop to ask, assumed resistance, and—didn't know. Perhaps his pleasure was in the killing and not the sex."

"Oh my God," Shirley said.

"She must have been a very handsome, very sexy-looking woman," Hardy said. "Incidentally, the door wasn't forced. Whoever came in, she let in."

"Sounds in character," I said.

"Probably someone she knew," Hardy said.

"I don't understand what she was doing with a suite here," Shirley said. "She has a duplex on Park Avenue, only a few blocks from here."

"She was chairman of the Cancer Fund Ball, coming up tonight," Hardy said. "There were a million details to handle. I suppose she wanted to be on the scene."

"So a lot of people must have been coming and going," I said. "She wouldn't have hesitated to answer the doorbell without finding out first who it was. She expected traffic."

"Makes sense," Hardy said. He looked at Shirley and smiled his pleasure again. "What can you tell me that are facts about Laura Kauffman, Miss Thomas? We can try the gossip on for size later."

Shirley took a couple of sheets of paper out of her briefcase. Laura Kauffman was evidently a big enough "wheel" in the social world for Shirley to have kept a file on her. There hadn't been time to type up these pages.

"She was born Laura Hemmerly," she said, glancing at her notes. "Jason Hemmerly, her father, was big steel. He died a couple of years ago and left Laura a very rich woman. Like a villa in the south of France, duplex on Park Avenue, something fancy in the Virgin Islands."

"What you call cosmopolitan," Hardy said.

"Good target for a thief," I said.

"But a butcher?" Hardy said, his pleasant face hardening. "About her husband, Miss Thomas?"

Shirley shifted pages. "Three of them," she said. "The first when she was sixteen. I don't have number one's name. He was a ski instructor somewhere in the Swiss Alps. This was in 1940, just before the big war."

Hardy's eyebrows rose. "That makes her fifty-three. I'd have thought she was quite a lot younger."

"Maybe she's been rebuilt," I said.

Shirley glanced at me. "You don't have to go to seed in your fifties," she said.

"You've got a long wait to find out," I said.

"The husbands, Miss Thomas," Hardy said.

Shirley went back to her notes. "As I say, I don't have the first one's name. It was something of a scandal. The usual suggestion that she was pregnant."

"But no child? No children ever?"

"No record of any. There was the war then, right after an annulment. Papa bought off the ski instructor, one guesses. Then there was the war and the Hemmerlys left their beloved Europe and came back to New York. Papa was making millions providing steel for tanks and guns and battleships. Laura spent her time, I gather, entertaining the armed forces. I use the word 'entertain' in a loose sense."

"I get the point," Hardy said.

"After the war Laura went hotfooting it back to Papa's villa in France. That's when she met and married Baron Siegfried von Holtzmann."

"Sounds rather German for the south of France at that time," Hardy said.

"Von Holtzmann was an unusual German," Shirley said. "Very blond, very handsome, with an eyeglass and a dueling scar. German army to the hilt, you'd say. But he spent the war underground, the story goes, dedicated without success to destroying Hitler and his puppets. He did a lot, we are told, to help the French Resistance."

"Chambrun would know about him," I said. Only there was no Chambrun to ask.

"Von Holtzmann has no connection with this," Shirley said. "In 1953, after five years of marriage to Laura, he blew his brains out in a hotel room in Paris. He left Laura with his title and apparently no explanation for his self-destruction."

"That's twenty-five years ago!" I said.

Shirley nodded. "The year I was born," she said.

So now I knew—about Shirley.

"For twenty years after that," Shirley went on, "Laura became *the* hostess in the swinging social set. New York, Paris, Florence, Geneva, Acapulco. She has a place there, too. I grew up reading about her in the social columns. My first job as a reporter on a newspaper was covering her third wedding. That was seven years ago."

Shirley fumbled in her briefcase and came up with an eight-by-ten photograph. It was of a very lovely woman in a gorgeous wedding gown, attended by the groom, one James Kauffman.

"My God, she was forty-six," Hardy said. "She looks thirty."

"She had a secret a lot of us hope we have at her age," Shirley said.

"That's Kauffman?" Hardy asked. "He looks her age in the picture."

"You mean thirty? That's about what he was. Sixteen years younger. A stockbroker in Wall Street. He didn't belong in her set—the social set, I mean. I never did know how and where they met, but he was quickly indoctrinated. Photographs, news items, gossip tidbits.

I felt he was more like a faithful watchdog than a romantic husband. He dropped out of sight in Wall
Street. Why shouldn't he, with all her money? No
need to work. And then, a couple of years ago, he
dropped out of sight everywhere. Laura was seen with
other escorts. There was never any official announcement, he just sort of vanished. By then I was a prier,
what Mark calls a Peeping Thomas. I blush to tell you
that I tried to locate Jim Kauffman."

"Any luck?"

She hesitated. "In my business we are supposed to
be ruthless, Lieutenant," she said. "That means utter
disregard for privacy. I—I've never played it that way,
particularly when there is a tragedy below the surface."

"There is a tragedy involving Kauffman?" Hardy
asked.

"I suppose you have to find him," Shirley said.

"His wife has been murdered, Miss Thomas."

Shirley nodded. "Jim Kauffman has become a hope-
less alcoholic," she said. "A skid-row bum."

"She left him without money?"

"Maybe. Maybe he wouldn't take what she offered.
I found him down in the Bowery. He sometimes
sleeps and eats in a Salvation Army shelter down
there. I—I tried to talk to him but he didn't make
much sense. It was too painful to pursue it, and I
don't use that kind of thing in my column. I felt sorry
enough to want to help him, but he just turned his
back on me and walked away. Staggered away would
be nearer to the fact."

"Did he speak with any bitterness about his wife?"

"He wouldn't talk about her at all," Shirley said,

"which might be interpreted as a kind of bitterness, I suppose."

The phone rang and Hardy answered it.

"Oh, hello, Miss Ruysdale," he said. "No, it's pretty sticky so far. Yes, Jerry told me about the Man. I put out an all-points bulletin on him. Yes, he's here." He held out the phone to me.

"Mark, if you're not too involved, I could use you," Ruysdale said.

"No news of the Man?"

"None," she said. She sounded far away.

"I'm on my way," I said.

I left Shirley with Lieutenant Hardy to whom she was giving details about the Salvation Army shelter. I told her I would meet her in my apartment on the second floor when I could. She had a key to my place. After all, she was forever.

When I reached Ruysdale's office someone else was sitting at her desk. It was a girl from the secretarial pool named Charlotte something. I somehow couldn't remember her last name. She is a pretty sensational-looking chick and I once had my eye on her. After ten minutes' conversation with her over a drink in the Trapeze Bar one afternoon, I had stopped looking. Her measurements were sensational, but I discovered she was something less than half-witted when it came to casual conversation. Ever since then she had looked at me with sad spaniel eyes, as if she was wondering why the pass that had been obviously in the making had never come about.

"Miss Ruysdale is in Mr. Chambrun's office," Charlotte said. "You're to go straight in."

"Thanks," I said.

"Mark, is it serious about Mr. Chambrun?"

"Serious?"

"I mean, is he going to be fired?" Charlotte asked.

I was about to laugh at her when I realized she didn't know what was going on.

"I mean, with Mr. Garrity here—?"

"Who is Mr. Garrity?" I asked.

"Why, Mark, he's president of the syndicate that owns the hotel."

It may sound absurd, but I had never paid any attention to the names of people in the ownership group. Mayberry was the only one I knew by sight—and sound. Chambrun was the only person I paid any attention to at the top. The owners were faceless nonentities to me.

"I think it's unlikely Mr. Chambrun will get fired," I said, and went through the door to the inner sanctum.

Ruysdale was sitting at Chambrun's desk. I had never seen anyone but the Man sit there before. It jolted me some, yet if anyone was to stand in for him Ruysdale was it. She knew, I told myself, everything Chambrun knew about the operation of the Beaumont.

There were three men sitting in leather armchairs facing Ruysdale. Two of them I recognized as part of the film company outfit, though I didn't have names to go with their faces. The third man, by a process of elimination, had to be Garrity.

He was something else again. He was a big man with shaggy gray hair, in his sixties, I guessed. His face was jowly, lined, but the lines suggested humor. He had bristling gray eyebrows and under them were almost intolerably bright blue eyes. He watched me cross the room and before I reached the desk I had the feeling he had come to very thorough conclusions about me. This one, I told myself, was a genuine power-house.

"Thanks for coming, Mark," Ruysdale said. "This is Mr. Michael Garrity, president of the owners' syndicate."

Garrity raised a huge hand in a casual wave of greeting.

"This is Clark Herman, the producer of *Strategies,* the film that's being shot in the hotel," Ruysdale said.

Her man was a Hollywood type. Long, mod-styled dark hair, a gaudy blue and white sports jacket, a pink sports shirt, tieless, open at the throat, pale blue slacks, and sandals over pink and blue socks in a diamond pattern.

"Hello, Haskell," he said. They'd evidently been briefed on me before I arrived because Ruysdale hadn't mentioned my name.

I nodded and looked at the third man. He turned out to be one Chester Cole, public relations man for Herman Productions. He was more conventional as to clothes than his boss, wearing a dark gray business suit with a vest, white shirt and tie. A young man, slim, dark with the Hollywood touch of dark glasses in gold wire rims that hid his eyes and left him a sort of zero when it came to assessing him.

"There seem to be some problems in connection with the filming," Ruysdale said.

"Before we go into that I think it would be helpful if Mr. Haskell could bring us up to date," Garrity said. His voice was deep and strong.

"Jerry Dodd is doing everything possible to locate Chambrun," I said. "So far, nothing."

"That's sort of skipping over things, isn't it, Mr. Haskell?" Garrity said. "So far there is the Kauffman woman."

"I'm sorry," I said. "The police are trying to keep things quiet as long as possible—until they get some leads."

Garrity gave me a disarming smile. "Have you and they forgotten about George Mayberry, Haskell? By now the whole goddamned world knows that Laura Kauffman has been murdered in the Beaumont."

"That's right," I said. "He was going to the mayor and from there to the White House."

Garrity laughed, and it was a deep rumbling sound. "I pity the mayor and the president," he said.

"Mayberry has that much clout?" I asked.

"Mayberry has no clout at all," the big man said. "Just an enormous capacity for noise making."

"I thought perhaps you were here to haul Jerry Dodd up on the carpet," I said.

"I'll buy him a drink when he has time," Garrity said. "I'd have given anything to see someone puncture George Mayberry's pomposity. In fact, I've instructed Miss Ruysdale to keep that desk chair warm for Chambrun until we find him. I don't want Mayberry sitting there, even if it's just to have his picture taken. I am well aware, Haskell, that, while we own the real estate, the Hotel Beaumont is just another flophouse without Pierre Chambrun. So, about Mrs. Kauffman, please."

There wasn't really much to tell except the unpleasant clinical details of her murder. Hardy was on the trail of her absent husband. I supposed there would be a checkup of her Cancer Fund people to find out who had seen her last and when. There had been so much gossip about a rather sensational life that it was going to be hard to separate fact from fiction.

"Anyone who has been so delightfully scandalous in public usually has a private sector better hidden than most people's," I said. "There is probably a current boy friend who was about to get the gate. There may be one who had already gotten the gate and wanted to pay off Laura Kauffman."

"People with money, and she is loaded, acquire enemies who do not necessarily share their beds," Garrity said. "But the husband does look like a prime suspect, doesn't he? Down and out, broke, asked for help and got turned down. Carved her up in a drunken frenzy. It was in the papers that she was taking a suite here for a few days to supervise preparations for tonight's ball. Story handed out on purpose so people would know where to find her."

"Right," I said. "I released the story myself at the ball committee's request."

"You met Mrs. Kauffman?" Garrity asked, giving me a wise look.

"No. She was down on my calendar for a session before lunch."

Carl Herman, the film producer, cleared his throat. "We are very much concerned," he said. "Our camera people were to be on hand along with the press and television to film the ball. Our stars, Janet Parker and Robert Randle, were to slip in and dance with the crowd. Part of the footage for *Strategies*."

"So what worries you?" I asked.

"It would cost us a fortune in extras and costumes to restage the ball if it were called off."

"I don't think it will be called off," I said. "If it was a private party and not a charity ball, perhaps. But there are approximately a thousand people coming who have paid at least two hundred and fifty dollars a ticket in advance. Nobody is going to return that kind of money."

"That's a low estimate," Garrity said. "I paid fifteen hundred dollars apiece for my tickets, and a hell of a lot of others spent over the minimum."

"That makes me feel better," Herman said. "I know Mr. Chambrun was very much against our using the hotel for filming. Mayberry thinks he may just have gone off somewhere to sulk."

"Nonsense," Miss Ruysdale said.

"He was opposed to the filming, wasn't he?" Garrity asked.

"He was," Ruysdale said. "And quite justifiably in my opinion." She was a cool cookie.

"Why?" Herman asked. "Shooting a film as important as *Strategies* here would help promote the hotel."

"The Beaumont doesn't need that kind of promotion, Mr. Herman," Ruysdale said. "The Beaumont promotes itself by being what its guests expect it to be. That means that not five minutes' worth of service will be interrupted, that comings and goings will not be the food for your cameras—yours, Mr. Herman, or anyone else's."

"It would seem," Chester Cole said, speaking for the first time, his eyes hidden behind the black glasses, "that Mrs. Kauffman's privacy was invaded."

"In private," Ruysdale said.

"Why were we given permission if Chambrun was so opposed?" Cole asked.

"Because he was overruled by a stupid board of directors," Garrity said. "It would seem that your star, Miss Parker, has George Mayberry breathing hard. He pounded at us and hammered at us to overrule Chambrun, and we finally gave in just to shut him up. I will grovel in front of Chambrun and apologize when he turns up."

"You have a contract with us!" Herman said, his voice rising.

"Oh, I know, Mr. Herman. I'm just saying we should have listened to the man who knows. Mr. Haskell, keep me informed, will you?"

"Yes, sir," I said.

He pulled himself up out of his chair. It was like a lion rising from sleep. He was even bigger that I'd thought.

"Gentlemen," he said, "I think we'd better leave these people to the rather sticky business of keeping this hotel afloat until Chambrun comes back."

There were murmurs of thanks and they all left. Ruysdale had risen, and when we were alone she suddenly covered her face with her hands and I saw her shoulders heave. I went to her and put my arms around her.

"He'll show up, Betsy," I said. "Nothing or anyone can keep him away from here very long."

She was clinging to me then, crying softly. I held her until the storm passed. Then she looked up at me, dabbing at her face with a Kleenex. She gave me a crooked little smile.

"Well, hop to it, Haskell," she said. "We've got a hotel to run!"

Chambrun had said the same thing hundreds of times.

* * *

Chester Cole was waiting for me in the outer office when I left Ruysdale. He had taken off the dark glasses and was polishing them with a white linen handkerchief. His eyes were gray, pale, and suggested a kind of cynical amusement with the world. He put his glasses back on and folded the handkerchief neatly into his breast pocket, tips showing.

"This would seem not to be an ideal time to involve you with my problems," he said.

"It's my job to be of service if I can," I said.

"I get the feeling that the people who work for Chambrun really care for him," Cole said.

"We care," I said.

"I envy you," Cole said. "You see, I don't give a damn for the people I work for. Only the paycheck. That paycheck requires me to ask you to call on Claude Duval in his suite, Sixteen B, at your earliest convenience. In short, now."

"What does he want? Do you know?"

Cole's smile was sardonic. "That things run exactly his way tonight," he said.

I didn't have any taste for the filming of a movie at that moment. Cole knew that, I saw.

"Our Claude is a prime horse's behind," he said. "The great Duval is more important than anyone else on earth. He is a genius at what he does, but he is a sonofabitch. You'll need to have your temper buttoned down."

"Sonsofbitches are nothing new to me in this job," I said. "There is no good time to see him with things the way they are, so give him a call and ask him if now will do."

Claude Duval was something of a shock to me when I was ushered into his suite by a male secretary.

He was a dead ringer for the actor Telly Savalas, shiny bald, fringe of hair shaved tight to his skull. He even smoked a thin, black cigarillo. The likeness dissipated when he spoke. A cultured Brititsh accent shattered it.

"I appreciate your promptness, Mr. Haskell," he said. "I understand this is a troubled time."

He was wearing a plum-colored robe with a fur collar, probably mink. He hadn't risen from a throne-like armchair when I was presented. He waved to a small, straight-backed chair facing him. I chose to stand.

"Time is very precious at the moment," I said.

"It is also precious to me," he said, "and there are things to be rearranged. There are stipulations made by your missing manager which won't do at all."

"I'm sorry," I said. "I can't change any arrangements Mr. Chambrun has made without an okay from him."

"But you will have to, my friend," Duval said. "If Chambrun was available, I would make it clear to him that he has no choice. Since he isn't here, you will have to act for him."

I was tempted to tell him to stuff it, but I played the role of polite hotel employee. "If you would care to tell me what you want changed," I said.

"That is why I had you sent here," he said.

The secretary, a bespectacled nonentity, was suddenly at Duval's elbow with an ashtray. The genius flipped the ash off his cigarillo without looking.

"To begin with," he said, "the script calls for my two stars, Miss Parker and Mr. Randle, to be dancing together at a charity ball. We will need closeups of them, which means cameras will have to be moved out onto the floor, to follow them, to take closeups. Mr. Chambrun has had the impertinence to tell us that no cameras will be allowed out on the floor, only in the gallery where the news media cameras are stationed. He has gone further, stating that his security people will remove my cameras from the floor by force if we attempt to overrule his decision."

"Then that's what will be done," I said. "Obviously he didn't want the ball interrupted by something that isn't connected with it."

"My dear young ass!" Duval said. I suppose, at sixty, I in my thirties must have seemed young to him. "Do you realize what pleasure it will give the guests at the ball to be involved in a Duval spectacular?"

"I have no choice but to follow Chambrun's orders," I said.

"You think not?" he said. His eyes were cold as two newly minted dimes. "I have expressed my wishes to Mr. Mayberry and he has graciously agreed to rescind the rules. Mrs. Kauffman and her committee are quite agreeable. If Chambrun were here, he would certainly have to change his mind."

"But he is not here," I said. The casual way he'd mentioned Laura Kauffman suggested he didn't know what had happened in Twenty-one A. Maybe it wouldn't have made any difference to him if he did.

"God save me from having to deal with people who have no judgments of their own," Duval said. "Shall I have Mr. Mayberry join this conference, young man?"

"It's my understanding he's on the way to the White House for reinforcements," I said.

There was a slight tick at the corner of Duval's mouth. I guessed he was curbing an impulse to laugh. He must have known what an overblown phony Mayberry was.

"Your orders will come to you from the owners," he

said. "But I will continue to tell you what they will be. The second stipulation of Mr. Chambrun's which must be altered is that we may not use the lobby or the Trapeze Bar for filming unitl after four in the morning. At that time there will be no people in either place but the cleaning force. The place has to look real, as if it were functioning normally, Mr. Haskell. I repeat, no one will object to being involved in a Duval film. I want to begin filming at two thirty A.M. Not a moment later. I want to film people leaving the ball. I want to film real customers drinking in the Trapeze Bar."

"And Chambrun has said 'no'?"

"He had said 'no,' but Mr. Mayberry has said 'yes.'"

"I can't help you, Mr. Duval," I said.

"Then Mr. Mayberry will give the orders," he said.

"The problem will be to find someone to obey them," I said.

He stood up. He wasn't as tall as I'd imagined.

"Damn your impertinence," he said.

I'd had enough. "I'm sorry, Mr. Duval, but nobody in this hotel takes orders from anyone but Chambrun. If he has left orders, they will be carried out. If he comes back in time and changes his mind, that's another story. Until that happens I'm afraid you'll have to play by his rules."

"You little pipsqueak bastard!" he said.

"The best I can do is try to find Chambrun and give you a chance to persuade him," I said. "I'd better get to that job now. Good morning, Mr. Duval."

THREE

Being shouted at by some self-important jerk like Duval didn't really bother me if I was sure of my ground. In this instance I hadn't had to make any decision of my own. Chambrun would be found. He had to be found. Meanwhile his instructions were law.

I went looking for Jerry Dodd. By now he must have come across something in the way of a lead, someone who had seen something or heard something.

His office is on the lobby floor, directly across from the registration desk. There is an intercom system between the security office and the desk clerk and also the cashier's window. It can be switched on from either end in case the desk clerk or the cashier want Security to overhear a conversation or Security is curious about someone.

I found Jerry Dodd in his office with Miss Kiley, the night chief operator on our switchboard. Miss Kiley had been at that job for twenty years. She had been the last person to speak to Chambrun every night during all that time.

Jerry looked at me with a suggestion of hope. Everyone had that look of hope this morning when they encountered someone they hadn't seen for a few minutes. Maybe that someone had some sort of news. I had none.

"Virginia tells me there was nothing unusual about the boss's sign-off last night," he said.

Virginia Kiley is a hard-faced woman whose only pleasure in life, I suspect, is her total efficiency at her job. She is proud of how she handles it and the trust placed in her by Chambrun.

"He says exactly the same thing every night," Kiley said. " 'No more calls, Miss Kiley, unless it's an emergency.' It could be a taped message, except it isn't."

"What time did he go up to the penthouse last night?" Jerry asked.

Kiley consulted a report sheet she had brought with her. "He checked with us at one fifteen," she said. "He was in the Spartan Bar. He told me he was on his way to the penthouse. Standard procedure. Seven minutes later he checked from the penthouse to tell me he was there. Nothing after that until the goodnight signal."

"Fifty-three minutes." Jerry said. "Were there any calls in or out in that time?"

"No."

"You could tell us from your chart exactly how he spent his evening?"

"I come on at seven o'clock," Kiley said. "He was in the penthouse then, according to Mrs. Veach's chart. He's almost always there when I come on, dressing for the evening. There were no calls until he checked with me at a quarter to nine. He told me he was on his way to his office for dinner. Six minutes later Miss Ruysdale called to say he was there."

Betsy Ruysdale's working hours coincide with Chambrun's.

"Miss Ruysdale monitors his calls when she's on the

job," Kiley said. "At quarter past nine there was a call
from Mr. Mayberry. We listen, you understand, to the
first few moments of all calls and then log them—who
the caller was and at what time."

"So he talked to Mayberry at quarter past nine?"

Kiley shook her head. "Miss Ruysdale wouldn't put
Mayberry through. He'd have to call back in an hour
when Chambrun finished dinner." Kiley gave us a
tight little smile. "Mayberry blew his stack, but Miss
Ruysdale wouldn't put him through."

"Go on, Virginia."

"At precisely ten o'clock Mr. Cardoza called. Miss
Ruysdale put him through so the boss evidently had
finished dinner."

Cardoza, the captain in the Blue Lagoon, would
know when Chambrun had finished dinner by checking with room service.

"While the boss was talking to Cardoza, Mr. Mayberry called back again. I told him the boss's line was
busy. He told me to cut in and I said I couldn't. He
told me he'd see to it that I was fired."

"I hope you didn't lose any sleep," I said. "He's
fired us all at least once today."

"I wasn't concerned," Kiley said. "I'd only have interrupted Mr. Chambrun for a bomb threat."

"And Mayberry is only a wet firecracker," I said.

"At twenty minutes past ten Miss Ruysdale called in
to say that Mr. Chambrun had gone to Miss Janet Parker's suite, Twenty-one C."

Jerry and I looked at each other. Three doors down
the hall from Laura Kauffman's last resting place.

"There weren't any calls for him. At eleven-oh-three
he called in to say he was in the Blue Lagoon. Twenty
minutes later he called to say he was 'making the

rounds' and could be reached in the Spartan Bar in about half an hour. In half an hour he checked in from the Spartan."

"A few minutes before midnight?"

"Eleven fifty-two. Nothing more until at one-fifteen he called to say he was on his way up to the penthouse."

"Making the rounds" was a routine which either Chambrun or I carried out every night, I, when he was tied up with something. It meant checking the bars, the restaurants, and any special rooms that were in use for special events, like balls, conventions, private dinners. I have said somewhere that it was like Marshall Dillon putting Dodge City to bed. I had guessed that the hour or more in the Spartan Bar had been spent playing backgammon with Dr. Partridge, the house physician. Doc Partridge is a crotchety old man, one of whose remaining dreams was to win a few bucks from Chambrun at a game he had no chance of winning. Chambrun was a terror at it.

So much for Chambrun's evening.

Jerry got on to Betsy Ruysdale when Miss Kiley left us. What did she know about Cardoza's call and Chambrun's visit to Miss Parker's suite? It seems they were related. Miss Parker, the star of Duval's film, had once, some years back, done a nightclub act which had played the Blue Lagoon. She had been a kind of present-day Helen Morgan, singing light, romantic songs. I remembered her when Ruysdale reminded us. The Blue Lagoon is an intimate room and Janet Parker, whose name had been something else at that time, had done very nicely in it. Miss Parker, it seemed, had called Cardoza, remembering him as a friend and a decent guy during the two weeks she'd

played the room. She told Cardoza she was being
given a hard time by some man in the hotel and what
should she do about it.

"Guess who the man is?" Ruysdale suggested.

"No time for guessing, Betsy," Jerry said.

Ruysdale laughed. "Mayberry," she said.

"Oh, God!" Jerry said.

"Since Mayberry apparently owns the hotel, according to Miss Parker, she didn't know how to handle the
situation," Ruysdale told us. "Cardoza told her how.
He'd have the boss come to see her. He went. That's
all I know, Jerry. I—I haven't seen him since."

The telephone log on Chambrun's comings and
goings the night before indicated nothing but a rather
ordinary evening. Jerry put in calls for Doc Partridge
and Mr. Quiller, the captain in the Spartan Bar. Doc
had gone out somewhere and Quiller wasn't due to
report for work until the cocktail hour that afternoon.
Mr. Cardoza, the elegant captain in the Blue Lagoon,
wasn't due till seven in the evening and he couldn't be
reached on a home phone they had for him.

The only thing with any substance about the evening was the rather absurd complication of Miss Parker's troubles with Mayberry whom she believed
"owned the hotel." A complaint about one guest mo-
lesting another was usually passed on to Jerry Dodd
to handle, but in this instance Chambrun had chosen
to take it on himself. Perhaps, I thought, because Cardoza had made a personal plea and Cardoza was one
of Chambrun's special people.

Jerry sat at his desk in the security office, doodling
on a scratch pad.

"Time of death in a homicide is a hard thing to be
precise about," he said. "Hardy tells me the Medical

Examiner's man thinks Laura Kauffman had been dead for from ten to twelve hours when they found her. That would place her killer in Twenty-one A between ten o'clock and midnight last night. The floor maid didn't go in to turn down her bed because there was a DO NOT DISTURB sign hung on the doorknob. But Chambrun was on the floor, only three doors away, between ten and eleven. It's possible he could have said something to the Parker girl, unimportant to her but important to us. I think I'd like to talk to her."

It was going on toward one o'clock that afternoon that Jerry and I went up to see the young movie star in Twenty-one C. The Beaumont was buzzing with the usual midday business. The governors had broken for lunch, disappointed when I told them Chambrun was still unavailable. Gussie Winterbottom, Claire De-Lune to you, was doing a land-office business with her new line of women's wear. The Cancer Fund Ball committee was in hectic session because of the tragic death of its chairperson—God how I hate that new word. They talked of cancelling the ball out of respect to Laura Kauffman, all the while looking a half million dollars straight in the eye.

"Laura would want us to carry on," they kept telling themselves. There really was never any doubt about carrying on.

And the Beaumont was swarming with news people. Jerry and I had used the freight elevator up to Twenty-one to avoid them. A couple of Hardy's men were in the hallway up there, checking on comings and goings. All the guests on the twenty-first floor had been questioned about last night. Who had gone to see Laura Kauffman or tried to see her. The last call to her room that she had answered had been a little before ten o'clock. After that, till well past midnight, there had been a dozen calls she hadn't answered. No one had been concerned about that. Laura Kauffman could have been, quite legitimately, anywhere.

Show business is a strange world, larded with luck. A young girl named Julia Parkhurst had started out as a singer in small nightclubs across the country. She had charm and not a little skill at the romantic and sentimental songs she sang. She had achieved something like real success when she was engaged to sing in the Blue Lagoon room at the Beaumont. It was there that some Hollywood big shot saw her. He decided, on the spot, that Julia Parkhurst was just the girl he wanted for a small part in a film he was casting. It didn't involve singing, but she had a special quality he wanted. She, of course, accepted the offer.

Why they changed her name to Janet Parker I don't know. Perhaps they didn't want her to be connected with a girl singer who had a minor reputation. The part was small but Janet made a big hit in it. She was nominated by the Academy for a best-supporting-actress award. She didn't get it, but she was now in demand. She had two leads after that which lifted her to the top of the ladder and now she was being starred in Claude Duval's latest. If it was as big a success as everyone anticipated, she was set for life.

Jerry and I got in to see her because, I guess, she had orders to see anyone who had "public relations" attached to his name. The filming at the Beaumont had gotten a lot of publicity and she was supposed to assist in exploiting it in any way she could.

She received us wearing a simple dark blue housecoat. Dark hair hung down to her shoulders. Her eyes were violet, like Elizabeth's Taylor's, but they weren't sophisticated. They seemed to ask for help, and I, for one, was instantly prepared to give it. That, I think, was her special charm, her special appeal.

She took us into her sitting room. This was a French suite, an exquisite Matisse on the wall over the mantel. All the people in Duval's company were in French suites.

"What can I do for you, Mr. Haskell? If it's about the unfortunate Mrs. Kauffman, I've already talked to the police. I had nothing to tell them."

"Mrs. Kauffman isn't our only problem today, Miss Parker," I told her. "Mr. Chambrun, our manager, is unaccountably missing. We understand he called on you last night."

"Missing?" Her eyes widened.

"He simply hasn't turned up for work this morning," I said. "Not having heard from him makes for concern."

"But of course."

"Can you tell us about his visit with you, Miss Parker?" Jerry asked.

She looked down at her slender hands.

"We know something about it, Miss Parker," I said. "Chambrun answered a call from Mr. Cardoza who was your friend when you worked in the Blue Lagoon as Julia Parkhurst."

"Mr. Cardoza is a very nice man," she said.

"And Chambrun is a very nice man," I said. "It was unusual for him to take on the kind of problem you evidently had. Mr. Mayberry?"

"It was very awkward," she said.

"You don't have to tell us, Miss Parker," Jerry said, "but it might be helpful if you would."

She looked up at me. "Mr. Mayberry is a disgusting creep," she said.

"Amen," I said.

"I'm not sure that you know," she said, "that the group that owns the Beaumont is heavily into financing Claude Duval's film."

That was something Chambrun had kept to himself, but it helped explain the hassle he'd had with the owners' syndicate over the filming. They undoubtedly felt they had the right to have one investment feed another. Chambrun's only concern would have been for the Beaumont and its image. The compromise had been restrictions on the filming that were driving Claude Duval up the wall.

"I was told by Mr. Herman and Mr. Duval when we checked in here that I should go out of my way to be nice to George Mayberry. He had, they told me, the power to make the filming here go smoothly."

I wondered what "being nice" to Mr. Mayberry meant. Janet Parker evidently read my mind, and there was a firm little set to her chin.

"Not what you're thinking, Mark," she said. First names came easy with her. "He called on me before I'd even gotten settled in these rooms. He brought flowers and a bottle of very old brandy. He said he'd been in love with me since he'd seen me in my first film. At first I thought it was cute, a man in his late fifties flirting with a girl young enough to be his daughter. Well, almost young enough!" Again the little jut of her chin. "After one pony of brandy he was all over me, trying to maul me. I tried to laugh it off and get rid of him. He insisted on dinner. I suggested the Blue Lagoon room. I knew Mr. Cardoza would be helpful if I needed help. In public the big ape would have to behave himself, I thought. I agreed to meet him there in half an hour. Once I was rid of him I tried to reach Mr. Herman, our producer. I found him in Duval's suite."

"You didn't have to keep your date with Mayberry," I said.

"That's what I thought," she said. "I wanted Clark Herman to handle it for me. He sounded distressed. He said something to Duval I couldn't hear and then he put Duval on the phone. Nothing in the world matters to Claude except having his own way. He made it very clear to me. He needed Mayberry's help to handle the 'stupid bastard of a manager' who was throwing roadblocks in the way of filming. 'Can it matter so much to let him have a few feels and maybe a little necking? You're a big girl, Janet, and we need your cooperation. Play along. You have to be ready for shooting the ballroom sequences around midnight. You can stall him, promise him anything for later. Later we will have gotten our way with Chambrun and you can tell Mayberry to drop dead.' " She drew a long breath. "Starring in a Duval film, maybe others in the future, is very important to me. So—so I met Mayberry in the Blue Lagoon as I'd promised."

"Nice business you're in, Miss Parker," Jerry said.

"Let's face it," she said, "there are hundreds of opportunities to advance your career by 'being nice' to someone, agents, directors, producers, male stars." She gave me a bitter little smile. "I have managed to avoid most of that kind of thing. I wasn't about to have any part of George Mayberry."

"But you kept your date," Jerry said.

"Yes, and you wouldn't believe. The minute we were seated by Mr. Cardoza, who was very glad to see me, Mayberry was under the tablecloth, groping for my leg, my thigh, other areas. I think he expected me to light up and swoon with delight. I—I wanted to vomit in my soup. I kept telling him that a working night was ahead of me; I had lines to make sure of, the makeup people would need to prepare me a couple of hours before the rehearsal. Later, I told him, tomorrow, meaning today, when the filming was done—"

"Bastard!" I said. "But the filming isn't until tonight."

"Rehearsals," Janet said. "I told him I wouldn't be able to do anything but concentrate on my job until after the filming tonight. Then, I let him believe, my time would be my own—and his. He kept slobbering that he couldn't wait, that he'd been waiting all his life for me—junk like that. Finally, mercifully, he had to go to the john. I signaled to Mr. Cardoza and he came over to the table. I told him what was cooking. He was very angry. He told me if I could stall Mayberry until ten o'clock he would call Mr. Chambrun. Chambrun, he said, was the one person who could handle Mayberry."

Cardoza knew that Chambrun wouldn't have finished his dinner till ten o'clock. You could tell time by that routine.

"At ten o'clock Mr. Cardoza came back to the table," Janet said. " 'Mr. Chambrun wonders if he could see you in your suite for a few minutes,' he said. 'What the hell for?' Mayberry wanted to know. 'Something about the filming,' I said. So I got away. A few minutes later Mr. Chambrun arrived here. He's a charming man."

"I know," I said. That little knot was tightening in my stomach. Where the hell was he?

"He was very gracious," Janet said. "He was angry, too. He told me not to worry about Mayberry. He'd take care of him, he said. Then he stayed and talked with me for about twenty minutes, about films, about music. I guess I'd acted as though I was in shock, but by the time he was ready to go, I was relaxed, had literally forgotten about my troubles. A delightful man. What can have happened to him?"

"I wish to God I could tell you," Jerry said.

"There's one thing more, quite crazy," Janet said. "I went to the door with Mr. Chambrun when he was leaving. He had phoned the switchboard to say he was going to make rounds. Pleasant reassurances from him. Just then a door opened up the hall and Mayberry came out of Suite Twenty-one A. I didn't know then that it was Mrs. Kauffman's suite. Chambrun gave me a wicked little smile and said something about the fates doing away with delay. He called out 'Mayberry!' and I closed the door. I—I didn't want to witness the encounter."

Jerry glanced at me, his face tense. "You told this to the police?" he asked her.

She nodded. "They've questioned everybody on this floor."

Lieutenant Hardy had taken over Chambrun's office on the second floor. Chambrun would have wanted it that way. He would have been present had he been available. He and Hardy worked well together. The lieutenant was a slow, plodding, very me-

thodical man who never missed a single inch of the
trail along the way; Chambrun was instinctive, a brilliant hunch player, and he knew his hotel as no cop
knew his own city. Unfortunately he wasn't there to
add his own kind of genius, let alone facts he must
have that we all wanted desperately to know.

I almost felt sorry for George Mayberry when Jerry
and I found him closeted with Hardy when we came
down from Janet Parker's suite. The big man was in
real trouble. He must have been one of the last people
to see Laura Kauffman alive. He had had a confronta-
tion with Chambrun about two hours before Chambrun had disappeared off the face of the earth. He
was the only lead Hardy had, and the lieutenant was
bearing down hard.

Hardy turned away from Mayberry as we came in,
and his unspoken question was answered without
words. No news of Chambrun.

"We've just come from talking to Janet Parker,"
Jerry said. "We know from her that she saw Mayberry
come out of Mrs. Kauffman's suite shortly before
eleven last night. Chambrun was with Miss Parker,
and he was headed for a talk with Mayberry."

"I have been asking for explanations." Hardy said.

The office was pleasantly air conditioned, but Mayberry was mopping at a very red face with a handkerchief.

"You are asking me about personal matters that I
don't have to answer," he said.

"Let's forget about Chambrun for the moment,"
Hardy said. He knew that, whatever had passed between Mayberry and Chambrun, Chambrun had
spent another hour or more in the Spartan Bar afterwards. "But you are a material witness in the Kauff-

man case, Mr. Mayberry. The Medical Examiner tells
us she died between ten o'clock and midnight. You
were seen coming out of her suite at about ten minutes to eleven. You can tell us about your visit to Mrs.
Kauffman as any innocent man might, or you can
force me to get a warrant for your arrest as a material
witness, and you are entitled to have your lawyer present."

"Laura—Mrs. Kauffman—was perfectly fine when I
left her," Mayberry said. "It was a social visit. She was
an old friend."

"I don't have time for bullshit, Mr. Mayberry,"
Hardy said.

Mayberry waved his hands like a drowning man
reaching for a life preserver. "It had to do with the
ball, and the filming that's to take place tonight," he
said.

"So take your time, but tell it all," Hardy said.

"Mr. Chambrun was being unreasonable about the
filming tonight," Mayberry said. He looked at me, and
then at Jerry, as if he expected one of us to defend the
boss. Neither of us said a word. "It had been agreed
that the two stars, Mr. Randle and Miss Parker, could
be filmed dancing at the party. But Chambrun refused
to allow cameras on the floor, only in the gallery
where the news cameras will be. There'd be no way to
get good closeups that way, or move around to get the
closeups from different angles."

"Don't they have something called a zoom lens that
will take a closeup from a distance?" I asked.

"Duval won't hear of it. This isn't some action
event. It's a sensitive and artistic handling of a love
story. He couldn't get the effects he must get. Chambrun's claim is that it would interfere with the plea-

sure of the guests who have paid high prices for their tickets as a contribution to the Cancer Fund. I went to see Laura—Mrs. Kauffman—to get her to use her influence to change Chambrun's mind."

"Your syndicate owns the hotel, doesn't it?" Hardy asked. "Couldn't you just give orders?"

"We have a contract with Chambrun," Mayberry said. "It gives him a final authority on all details connected with management."

"It makes it sticky," I said. "It seems Mayberry and his friends have invested in Duval's film."

"Something like two million dollars," Mayberry said. "Surely it's not unreasonable to expect some consideration from Chambrun. If the ball people didn't mind, why should he?"

"So you went to see Mrs. Kauffman," Hardy said. "When?"

"I was dining with Miss Parker in the Blue Lagoon," Mayberry said. "She had to leave about ten—to rehearse, or something. I called Laura when Miss Parker left and she invited me up."

"A few minutes after ten?"

"Yes."

"So you went up."

"Yes. We had a couple of drinks while I told her about our problem with Chambrun. She'd already discussed it with her ball committee. Frank Herman and Duval had been to see her."

"Last night?"

"She—she didn't say. I didn't ask. All that mattered to me was that the committee was perfectly willing to allow a movie camera on the dance floor. They thought people would be fascinated to be part of a filming. She agreed to talk to Chambrun."

"And did she?"

"She tried to get him on the phone but they weren't able to locate him."

"You knew he was next door in Janet Parker's suite," I said. "The captain in the Blue Lagoon told Miss Parker he was on his way in your presence."

"Yes, I knew that," Mayberry said, giving me a murderous look. "I thought she might be using her influence for Herman and Duval; not a good time to interrupt."

"But you met Chambrun just as you were leaving Mrs. Kauffman's suite. You brought that matter up with him?" Hardy asked.

"He seemed to take delight in making things difficult. He said he didn't give a damn what the committee felt about it. He said he'd have to have a clearance from every one of the hundreds of guests present before he'd allow a camera on the floor. He said if they'd paid money to be part of a filming that was one thing, but since they'd paid to attend a ball, a ball was what they were going to get."

"He had a point," Hardy said.

"But we own the hotel, and we have an investment in the film!"

"Probably a very shrewd use of your funds," Hardy said. "Let's go back to Mrs. Kauffman."

"There's nothing to tell except what I've told you."

"I think there is. You say she's an old friend. How long have you known her?"

"About fifteen years, I'd say. I've dined at her apartment here in town, visited her at her villa in the south of France, spent a weekend at her place in Acapulco. Old, good friends."

"You know her husband?"

"Jim Kauffman? Of course I know him."

"I understand they're separated."

Mayberry shrugged, as if the movement helped relax his personal tensions. "For some months now, I think. I've taken Laura to the theater a few times. She hasn't wanted to talk about it, but I had the feeling the marriage was permanently on the rocks."

"What kind of a man is he?"

"Jim? A pleasant enough fellow, but is was a little hard for him to keep up with Laura's pace."

"Pace?" Hardy asked.

"She had three or four houses, always on the move. Liked to play hostess to all the rich and famous. Jim, I think, would have liked to settle down and take it easy."

"He had no money of his own?"

"I don't think so; not when he stopped working on Wall Street. But, hell, Lieutenant, he didn't need money. Laura was so rich it hurts to think about it."

"We know that Kauffman has become an alcoholic," Hardy said. "He's apparently without funds, down on skid row somewhere."

"I'm sorry to hear that," Mayberry said.

"You didn't know?"

"No."

"Do you know if Mrs. Kauffman offered to make a settlement of some sort on him?"

"No."

"It would have been decent of her, wouldn't it? He'd given up his job to toddle around after her."

"What was between them was none of my business," Mayberry said.

"Did Mrs. Kauffman mention him to you last night?"

"I don't recall that she did."

"Think," Hardy said. "Did she tell you he was coming to see her. She might, since you were such an old friend."

"I'm sure she didn't." Mayberry's eyebrows rose. "My God, you're not suggesting that Jim Kauffman—?"

"I cover every possibility, Mr. Mayberry."

I suddenly thought about Shirley. I was very late for the lunch I'd promised her. From what she'd told us about Laura Kauffman, and what Janet Parker had told us about Mayberry, I had the feeling he wouldn't have hung around the lady for fifteen years just to spend a weekend at Acapulco. Hardy was right with me.

"Were you one of Mrs. Kauffman's lovers?"

Mayberry sat straight up in his chair as though there was an electric charge in it. "That's none of your goddamned business!" he said.

"All of Mrs. Kauffman's lovers are my business today," Hardy said.

Mayberry mopped at his face with his handkerchief. "She was a widow for the first ten years I knew her," he said. "We—we may have had a few intimate moments, but that was long ago. She was a damned attractive woman."

"Not any more," Hardy said, his voice grim. "I'm going to get the man who butchered her, Mr. Mayberry."

"I certainly hope so."

"So let's go back to Chamburn," Hardy said. "You met him in the hall outside Mrs. Kauffman's suite. You discussed the camera-at-the-ball situation?"

"I told you. He was unreasonably stubborn about it."

"What else did you talk about?"

"Nothing, that I can recall."

Jerry got into the act then. "Mayberry had been offensive to Miss Parker," he said in a flat voice. "She asked Cardoza for help and Cardoza called the boss. Chambrun went up to Twenty-one C to assure Miss Parker she didn't have to worry about Mayberry any more. Surely Chambrun must have brought it up. When he saw Mayberry in the hall he told Miss Parker that the fates were doing away with delay."

"You really must hate his guts," Hardy said.

"The whole thing is absurd," Mayberry said. "Actresses like Miss Parker expect to have passes made at them. Disappointed if you don't. She's a—"

"—damned attractive woman," Hardy said.

"All she had to do was say no!" Mayberry said.

"Maybe not," Jerry said. "She was being pressured by Herman and Duval to be nice to you, at least until after the filming."

"I don't need help from anyone!" Mayberry said.

"I have a feeling you may need a hell of a lot of help before we're through here," Hardy said.

I went down the hall to my apartment. It was nearly three o'clock and I wasn't surprised to find Shirley gone. There was a note propped up on the mantel.

I'm not mad, luv, [it read] but with big stories all around I just couldn't sit here. Later I have to get dolled up for the ball so that you won't be able to look at anyone else. I hope Chambrun will show up with some simple explanation, oth-

erwise I may not be able to seduce you. Love, luv.
Shirley.

That one is special. I was just about to leave to
make the rounds of the governors and the fashion
show and the preparations in the main ballroom when
there was a heavy knock on my door. It was Doc Partridge, the house physician. He is a craggy, shaggy old
gent, but a friend, particularly a friend of Chambrun's. He looked shaken.

"What's this about Pierre?" he asked.

I told him. No word, no sign of Chambrun since his
"no more calls" to Miss Kiley at two fifteen. No message, no demands from potential kidnappers. And
now, after hours of grinding search, no trace of him so
far anywhere in the Beaumont, nor any response to
the all-points bulletin Hardy had put out on him.

"If he had wanted to disappear, he'd be delighted
at how perfectly he'd managed it," I said.

"Of course he didn't want to disappear! That's nonsense!" Doc nodded toward a chair. "Mind if I sit
down, Mark? I feel a little unsteady."

"Give you a slug of something?" I asked.

"This is a time to keep your wits about you," he
said.

"I take it you spent some time with Chambrun in
the Spartan last night?"

"Midnight till a little after one," Doc said. "Sonofabitch threw more doubles than you could imagine.
Decent people shouldn't be allowed to play backgammon with him."

"Was there anything unusual about him last night,
Doc? Did he seem tense, or nervous, or distracted?"

"Not so distracted that he couldn't concentrate on beating my brains out," Doc said.

The Spartan Bar is one of the last bastions of male chauvinism in the city. Not long ago it had been clearly marked to indicate that women were not admitted. There are no signs these days but there are subtle ways to let ladies know that they aren't welcome. Its principal patrons are elderly gentlemen who sit around at tables playing chess, backgammon, and gin. And drinking. Doc Partridge, whose practice now is only the emergency care of hotel transients, spends most of his time in the Spartan, mourning with his cronies all the things of elegance and pleasure that had once made up his world and theirs. I wouldn't for the world have told Doc that Chambrun had discussed a future for the Saprtan Bar that would totally change it. Old-timers like Doc couldn't go on forever. They were already thinning out.

"You don't hand around the Spartan very much," Doc said, giving me a hostile look. "Things don't change very much there."

"My time will come," I said.

"When you time comes it will have changed," Doc said. "Thank God I won't be here to see it. There is one thing that never changes. Pierre shows up there around midnight every night. Sometimes he stays, sometimes, when he's needed somewhere else, it's just to say hello. It reassures us old codgers. Our world is on an even keel as long as Pierre is around. We need to know it."

"So he came in last night to reassure you," I said, prodding him gently.

"Nothing different. He was mad as hell about

something. That's par for the course. He's always mad as hell about something. He's just finished his rounds, you see, and he's always found something out of place, someone not doing his job up to Chambrun standards, maybe some finger marks on a bar glass in the Trapeze. 'You got an instant prescription for high blood pressure?' he asked me last night. 'I feel inclined to commit a murder, Doc.' I asked him who and he said: 'Oh, to hell with it. Where's the backgammon board?'"

"That was it? No more talk about what made him angry?" I knew Chambrun had had his encounter with George Mayberry not too long before that. It would have explained his anger.

"While we were setting up the board," Doc said, "he muttered something about 'that goddamned film company' that was going to disrupt things. That's tonight, isn't it? And something about 'the brainless owners.' Then he grinned at me, handed me a dice cup, and said, 'Go, sucker!' That was all. He plays any game—chess, gin, backgammon, billiards—as if his life depended on it. The only thing on his mind for the next hour and a half was skinning me alive. Which he did."

"A medical question, Doc," I said. "We've been concerned that he might have had a heart attack, a stroke, with nobody around—in some room we haven't searched yet, some closet or storage space."

Doc snorted at me. "Pierre? Pierre is fifty-eight years old but he has the heart of a boy of twenty. You should envy his blood pressure. For all his blusterings and displays of anger I've never known a man with fewer tensions. He's in perfect shape for a man much younger than he is."

"It's good to hear," I said, "but it doesn't cheer me up. It makes the chance of some kind of violence greater."

"If anyone has harmed him," Doc growled, "I will end my life by killing the sonofabitch who did it!"

I guess a lot of us felt that way.

It is difficult to describe how that day wore on. Jerry Dodd and his men carried on the slow, grim search of the hotel. They would not have covered all the ground for hours and hours. But as time ticked away those of us who knew what they were searching for were plunged deeper and deeper into a kind of fatalistic despair. They weren't going to find Chambrun.

Nothing was normal as the day wore on. A lot of us knew about Chambrun but the word hadn't leaked to the press. However, we had a murder that had leaked, and the place was swarming with reporters and photographers trying to get some kind of newsbreak from Hardy. They had deadlines to meet, and facts were sparse. Laura Kauffman had been stabbed to death in her suite. The police were following rather slender leads. That was all they got.

About four o'clock I met with Ruysdale and Michael Garrity in Chambrun's office. The big man, who was really the power in the owners' group, turned out to be reasonable and stubborn at the same time. He thought at first that to throw the Chambrun story into the news hopper might draw attention away from the murder. Ruysdale and I easily persuaded him that to do that would turn the hotel into bedlam. Reporters would instantly hint at two murders. It was finally agreed that I would meet with reporters, repre-

senting the hotel. It would be my job to persuade
them that Laura Kauffman's murder had nothing to
do with a breakdown of hotel security. She had, in
effect, had an office here to handle ball arrangements. People were free to come and go. No one had
broken into the room. Whoever it was had been let in
by Mrs. Kauffman. There hadn't been any reason at
all to keep the lady under surveillance or guarded.
Hotel security was cooperating with the police in every way possible. The theme, then, was that the Beaumont's management had no reason to feel responsible
for what had happened.

Michael Garrity was not so pliable in another area.
He expressed himself in rather colorful language on
the subject of George Mayberry.

"When the police get through with him," Garrity
said, in his deep rumbling voice, "I'll see to it that the
stupid bastard is kept out of the hotel—from here on
in. Which brings us to the ball and the film."

"Mr. Chambrun had laid out very specific rules and
regulations," Ruysdale said. She was sitting at Chambrun's desk again, and she looked exhausted, deep
dark circles under her eyes.

"I'm aware of that," Garrity said. "But I think if
Chambrun were here, I could persuade him to change
his mind about those rules. You see, Miss Ruysdale, the
ball will no longer be an elegant charity affair. A
thousand people will be jabbering about rape, and
murder, and violence. Very damaging to the hotel for
months to come. The one thing that might divert
them, give them something else to talk about and
think about, would be a filming on the dance floor
and later in the lobby and the Trapeze Bar while people are still here. Duval is a famous man, like a Berg-

man or a Fellini. He will put on a show for them, involve them, use them. They will go home talking about him and not the unfortunate Mrs. Kauffman. I think it's just good sense to permit the diversion, where under normal conditions it might have been as objectionable as Chambrun thought it would be."

It made some sense, I thought.

"If Mr. Chambrun comes back and finds we've gone over his head—" Ruysdale said.

"He's a reasonable man," Garrity said. "When he understands the reasons for overriding him, he may award us all the order of merit."

Ruysdale looked at me. For once I thought she was too done in to think clearly for herself.

"I think Mr. Garrity's made a case," I said. "I buy it."

And so it was that Claude Duval got his way. Ruysdale and Garrity would notify him and make whatever arrangements had to be made to suit him. I went off to meet the press, hastily assembled in one of the small dining rooms off the lobby.

I think I made my case, that the hotel was not responsible for what had happened to Laura Kauffman. I had no facts for them because I had no facts. Among those present was that old chicken hash connoisseur, Eliot Stevens. As the session broke up I found him waiting for me in the lobby.

"Quite a day," he said.

"Quite a day," I said.

"Did Chambrun ever show up?" he asked.

"With endless apologies for you," I said, lying as blandly as I could.

He gave me a narrow-eyed smile. "Have it your way," he said. "I'm willing to sit on that story in the hope of getting a big one from him later. One question, just between us. Is there any connection between the Chambrun disappearance and the Kauffman case?"

"If I could answer that, it would mean I knew what has happened to Chambrun," I said. "At this moment we haven't a notion. That's just between us, Eliot."

"With the guarantee that I get first crack at the story when it breaks."

"A deal," I said.

He looked around the busy lobby. People were crowding into the bars early. It wasn't business as usual. Everyone was trying to pump the doormen, the bellboys, the bartenders, any other identifiable members of the staff. Who killed her? Why?

"Does it occur to you that you may have a sex maniac running wild in your hotel?" Stevens asked me.

"Eliot, everything has occurred to me but the answer," I said.

I had, literally, to fight my way across the lobby to the elevators. Regular customers and most of the Beaumont's guests know me by sight. If anyone could tell them something juicy, I was it. I thought I was going to get my clothes torn off, like some movie star caught out by his fans, before I got to the elevator and the safety of the second floor.

I walked along the second floor corridor, mercifully deserted, to the door of my apartment and let myself in. I had company. Shirley was there, the only other person who had a key, and with her was a man I didn't know. He was in his middle thirties, I thought, fishbelly pale, sick-looking really. He wore a seedy gray flannel suit that I recognized had cost a lot of money when it was new. Shirley looked very serious.

"Forgive me for barging in, Mark," she said. "This is Jim Kauffman."

The dead woman's husband! I understood the ghostly pallor now, the unsteady hands, the faint tick at the corner of his mouth. This character was in the grip of a monumental hangover. Red-rimmed eyes looked despairingly from me to the little portable bar in the corner of my living room. This one was right on the verge of falling into a thousand pieces. I shook hands with him, and it was like taking hold of something dead.

"I didn't know who else to go to for help, Mark," Shirley said.

"Help?" I said.

Kauffman sat down because it was obvious his legs wouldn't hold him up any longer. He raised a hand to try to control the twitching of his mouth. Shirley was eyeing me with a peculiar steadiness, more like a stranger than a lover.

"I went to find Jim," she said. "I knew Hardy would be looking for him and I thought it was only fair to prepare him. After all, I sort of turned him in."

True, I thought.

"When he told me his story I knew he'd never stand up under questioning by the cops. What to do? That's why I brought him here, Mark."

"Right through the lobby?"

"Nobody would know me the way I look now," Kauffman said, in a hollow voice. He looked up at me. "I—I was here last night. I—I saw her."

"Well, why not? You're her husband," I said.

He took in a kind of gasping breath. "After she was dead," he said. "Oh, Jesus, Mr. Haskell, could I have just a little slug of your scotch?"

I felt a cold chill run right down my back. "I think you better tell me about it first," I said. One good drink and he'd probably pass out right here on my rug. Shirley was in trouble, I thought, harboring a suspect from Hardy. Because, God knows, Kauffman was a suspect.

He didn't look at me, just at the scotch bottle. "Miss Thomas has told you about me," he said. "I'm shot, shot all to hell."

"I can see that," I said.

"Sometimes, when you're in my kind of shape," he said, "nothing matters to you except—except getting what you need, liquor. Not pride, not anything. Last night was like that."

I waited for him to go on. His whole body shook with the desperate need for what was in that scotch bottle. "Laura and I have been separated for about ten months," he said. He had a pleasant voice, an easy way of talking if he hadn't been so beat. I could see that he had been an attractive guy—once upon a time. "I could never supply her with what she needed," he went on. "No one man ever could. After a while I—I couldn't stand having to knock on the door of her bedroom before I went in, to be sure there wasn't someone else with her. So I walked. Oh, please, Mr Haskell!"

"Keep talking," I said.

"She offered to make a settlement on me, but I wasn't having any of that. I was going to be a man, for a change, stand on my own two feet." He laughed, a bitter sound. "My God! I'd been boozing it quite a bit by the time I walked out on her and I found—it was all I cared about. It—it's come to this! What little money I had went quickly. Then I began to steal a

little, and con people. And then—then last night—I
was at the very bottom of the well."

"So you came here?"

"I'd read in the paper that Laura had taken a suite
at the Beaumont to handle the Cancer Fund Ball. I
called her, the first time I'd talked to her since—in ten
months. I said I was desperate, needed help. She told
me to come to see her. It was about eleven o'clock at
night then. It was after midnight when I got here, perhaps twelve thirty. So I went up to Twenty-one A. I—I
was out of my mind with need then, Haskell. Physically, the walk had just about finished me. I—I rang
her doorbell and she didn't answer. I knocked. Nothing. Then I guess I blew my stack. I started pounding
on the door, shouting at her. It should have raised
the whole floor full of people."

"The suites on twenty-one are all soundproofed," I
said.

"I was pounding and yelling," Kauffman said, "and
then I realized the door wasn't latched! I went
charging in. She wasn't there. But there was a sideboard loaded with liquor. I just about made it and
poured myself a whole glass of scotch. It—it works
very quickly on me."

"I can imagine," I said.

"I—I was suddenly full of fantasies," Kauffman said.
His voice was shaking now. "She was in the next
room, in the hay with some guy, paying no attention
to me. I didn't knock. I just charged in. And there—oh
my God, there she was. Bloody, dead, destroyed!
Now, Haskell, please!"

I was shaken myself. I walked very slowly toward
the bar. From there I faced him. "And then?" I said.

"The room looked like a slaughterhouse," he said. "Blood everywhere. I—I just turned and ran, stopping to grab a bottle of liquor from the sideboard."

"You didn't call the police or anyone?" I asked.

"All I wanted was to get out of there!" Kauffman said. "That jolt of scotch I'd had—I thought I was having a nightmare. I—I've had them, horror dreams. What I'd seen couldn't be real. All I wanted to do was get out of there and blot out the world."

"So you just took off and left her there?"

"I wasn't a block away before I was convinced the whole thing was a crazy, liquor-induced hallucination," Kauffman said. "I got back to my hole on the Bowery and—and drank enough of the scotch I'd taken to pass out. When I came to late this morning I *knew* it had been a nightmare. Then—then I went to the Salvation Army center for a cup of coffee. They had a radio going and I heard the news. It was real. What I had seen was real!"

He slumped forward in his chair and I thought he was going to topple out of it. I poured a good-sized drink for him that must have seemed inadequate to him. He swallowed it like water down a drain pipe. He trembled and shook and made an effort to pull himself together.

"You went looking for him?" I asked Shirley.

"I knew the cops would be hunting for him," she said. "I thought he'd need a friend. I thought if he'd come in, voluntarily, you might be able to persuade Lieutenant Hardy to deal with him gently. If the cops went to work on him, they'd simply drive him up the wall. He's a very sick man, Mark."

Sick enough to butcher his wife if she turned him

down, I thought. Sick enough not to be certain whether he'd done it or not. He was living in what someone has called Nightmare Alley.

"You're going to have to talk to Lieutenant Hardy," I told Kauffman. "You're going to have to do it now, not some other time."

"Oh, God!" he said, and held out his empty glass to me.

"After you've seen Hardy," I said.

Hardy was where I had last seen him, in Chambrun's office, going over reports from the fingerprint people, the police photographers, and the medical examiner. I told Hardy about Kauffman. Hardy listened, controlling his impatience.

"So bring him down here," he said.

"Couldn't you talk to him in my place?" I asked. "With Shirley there, and me, he may not cave in on you. He thinks of us, Shirley at least, as friends. He's pretty near the edge of the cliff."

"Okay, mother Haskell," Hardy said, giving me a tired smile. He reached for the phone. "I'd better have a police stenographer present."

"When he's ready to make a statement," I said, "try treating him like a human being, not as if you were the public executioner. It's your best chance with him."

Hardy, for all his official efficiency, is a decent guy. He's also a pretty good psychologist. I remembered him talking a potential suicide off a window ledge on the top floor of the Beaumont some years ago. I knew he had the skills to talk to a disturbed person like Kauffman without trying to bludgeon him for facts.

Kauffman looked at the detective with a kind of

cornered-animal panic in his bloodshot eyes when Hardy faced him.

"Thanks for coming in, Mr. Kauffman," Hardy said.

It was a good beginning.

Kauffman shook his head from side to side. "I didn't know what to do, Miss Thomas persuaded me—" It drifted off.

"Miss Thomas was right, of course," Hardy said. "Mr. Haskell has given me a brief account of what you've told him. I'd appreciate your telling it to me."

It was the same story, told a little more haltingly this time. When he came to the part where he'd decided it was all some kind of alcoholic dream, I could see that Hardy was growing impatient.

"So you weren't sure it was real till you heard the news on the radio this morning?" Hardy asked.

"I was sure it *wasn't* real till I heard the radio," Kauffman said. "My God, Lieutenant, you saw her! It was something out of a horror story."

"Yes, I saw her," Hardy said. He hesitated. "Is it possible, Mr. Kauffman, that in a moment of imbalance you could have attacked her and blotted it out of your memory?"

"My God, Lieutenant, I was wearing this suit! No one could have done that to her and not been covered with blood."

"You could have had it cleaned."

"Hell, I didn't have the money to take the subway back downtown," Kauffman said. "This is the only suit I have. I have some jeans and shirts, but this is the only suit. I wore it because I wanted to look the best I could for Laura."

"But you have had memory blackouts? It's not uncommon for people with your problem."

Kauffman twisted desperately in his chair. "Whole days go by sometimes—and I don't remember much of anything. But I don't have any reason to remember those days. I want to forget!"

"You could have wanted to forget what happened up there."

"It wasn't like that!" Kauffman cried out. "I tried to persuade myself it was a bad dream, but all the time I knew I'd seen it."

"Not done it?"

"No! No! No!" Kauffman protested.

"All right, Mr Kauffman," Hardy said, not unkindly. "Let's try for some other details."

"Oh, my God!" Kauffman said. "Could I—could I have another drink? I just can't function without some help, Lieutenant."

Hardy nodded to me and I poured the poor bastard a modest slug and took it to him. He downed it in one gulp and handed back the empty glass. Hardy took up the questioning.

"You called your wife about eleven o'clock, you say?"

"Yes."

"She invited you to come see her?"

"Yes."

"You cleaned yourself up and walked all the way up from the Bowery. When did you get here?"

"I don't have a watch," Kauffman said. "It's long gone in a hock shop. I can only guess it was quarter past, half past twelve."

"You called her on the house phone, you said. Did you get her room number at the desk?"

Hardy knew damn well the desk wouldn't give a room number out to anybody. They'd make a call for you but they wouldn't give out a room number to a stranger. "I'll see if Mrs. Kauffman is in," was the best they would do for him, even if he said he was her husband.

"Laura gave me the room number when I called her," Kauffman said.

"Then why didn't you go straight up to the room?"

"Because—oh, for God's sake, Lieutenant, hasn't anyone told you that Laura spent half her life in bed with other men. I didn't want to interrupt—something."

"But you went up when she didn't answer?"

"I was at the end of the line, Lieutenant."

"Did you see anyone in the hall on twenty-one?"

"No. I rang the bell. She didn't answer. I knocked. No answer. Then he began pounding and yelling."

"And you didn't see anyone?"

"I wasn't looking for anyone. There could have been ten people looking out of rooms at me and I wouldn't have seen them. All I wanted was to get in."

"And then you noticed that the door wasn't latched tight?"

"I was pounding on it and it—it just opened in a little."

"So you went in and there wasn't anyone there?"

"No one. No sign or sound of anyone. Then I saw the liquor. She had a supply there—for the people who were coming and going."

"There are fingerprints on bottles and glasses," Hardy said. "We've identified Mrs. Kauffman's. We haven't caught up with the others. What did you touch?"

"A bottle, a glass."

"What else did you touch?"

"Nothing. That's all I was interested in. You can't imagine how badly I needed a drink."

"I can imagine," Hardy said. "So after you'd had your drink you decided to investigate the bedroom?"

Kauffman gave him a bitter, trembling smile. "I was a big shot after I had that drink. I decided to break in. I expected to find her in the hay with some-one. I was going to tell her thanks for nothing, grab a couple of bottles, and take off."

"So you broke in and saw—?"

"My God, Lieutenant, you saw her! Do I have to describe it to you?"

"No," Hardy said. "You didn't try to see if she was still alive?"

"Alive in that condition?" Kauffman cried out.

"So you didn't touch her?"

"No!"

"Or anything in the bedroom?"

"*No!*"

"And then?"

"I just ran out. I grabbed a bottle off the sideboard and ran out."

"So you're out in the hall, bottle tucked under your jacket, I suppose. You see anybody then?"

"No. No, I ran to the elevator and rang, and it came."

"So the elevator operator saw you."

"It was self-service," Kauffman said. "There wasn't any operator."

Hardy gave me a questioning look.

"There are four elevators to that floor," I said. "After one o'clock only two of them have operators, the other two become self-service."

"So you pressed a button and went down to the

lobby," Hardy said to Kauffman. "There must have been people in the lobby."

"I suppose so," Kauffman said. "All I wanted to do was get out. I just went. Nobody tried to stop me or ask me anything. I walked back downtown. It seemed to take forever. I stopped in a few alleys to have a drink from the bottle. God help me, it was almost gone when I got back to my place."

"Your place?"

"I've been sleeping in the basement of a deserted house," Kauffman said. "I remember getting there, falling down on some rags I'd collected, and passing out. By then the whole thing was a drunken dream."

"And that's it?"

"That's it, Lieutenant." Kauffman looked longingly toward the glass in my hand.

Hardy fished a cigarette out of his pocket and lit it. "I ought to place you under arrest as a material witness, Mr. Kauffman," he said. He looked at me. "Is Doc Partridge available?"

"Round the clock," I said.

"So I am placing you under arrest, Mr. Kauffman, but I'm going to suggest that you stay here in the hotel's hospital under the care of Dr. Partridge, the house physician. Maybe he can give you some medication that will get you some sleep and help you dry out. It's your choice. Here or in a cell at the precinct house."

"There's no choice. Certainly you have to stay here," Shirley said. She reached out a hand to Kauffman's shoulder.

"I'd be glad to help," he said. It was an exhausted whisper.

* * *

My presence at the Cancer Fund Ball was a requirement of my job. I usually enjoy big parties
thrown at the hotel. The very rich and the famous are
always on hand. The women are always spectacularly
dressed and bejeweled. There were two bands for this
ball and they were society's darlings. With Shirley
looking like the brightest of stars to me, it should have
been a fun evening, but neither of us had any taste for
it. Her concern was for Jim Kauffman, lying sedated
in the hotel's infirmary, a cop guarding the door of his
room. Her concern was for him and for me. She knew
that nothing that was going on around us was of any
consequence to me, could in any way penetrate the
thick, dark gloom that had settled over me and the
other intimate members of the staff. Nothing whatever had turned up to explain Chambrun's disappearance. Jerry Dodd was at the point of being able to say
for certain that Chambrun was nowhere in the Beaumont, alive or dead. All the nonpublic areas of the
hotel had been searched. The last room-by-room
search of the guest accommodations was drawing to a
gloomy conclusion without result.

Early in the afternoon the FBI had come into the
picture. The agent in charge, one Frank Lewis, had
nothing to work with. A possible kidnapping was
what justified his presence, but there was only Chambrun's unexplained absence to suggest such an answer. He had been missing for some seventeen hours
when Lewis and two other agents showed up a little
after seven o'clock in the evening.

I had already changed into my dinner jacket when
Ruysdale called to ask me to come down the hall to
Chambrun's office. Lewis, the FBI man, was there

with her. He was a slim, dark young man with cool gray eyes behind wire-rimmed glasses.

"We haven't much to go on, Mr. Haskell," he said. "In a routine kidnapping we should have heard something by now; demands for money, something else they want. There has been nothing. There's no evidence of violence. Lieutenant Hardy has been over Chambrun's penthouse. It is just as the maids left it for him, bed turned down, pajamas laid out. We know he was there at two fifteen A.M. He called the switchboard to say he was turning in and would accept no calls except for an emergency. There were four or five cigarette butts in ashtrays, all the Egyptian brand Chambrun smokes. No others. We know, from the switchboard again, that he'd been in the penthouse for about an hour before that last goodnight call. Nothing forced, not the door, not the windows opening onto the roof garden outside. There are some fingerprints, mostly Chambrun's, a few identified as being the maid's. No others."

"Music?" Ruysdale asked, her voice husky from fatigue.

"There was a Beethoven symphony on the stereo system. Chambrun's prints on it."

"He—he always plays music when he's alone," Ruysdale said.

"So it comes down to this," Lewis said. "He announced to the switchboard that he was going to bed, but he didn't. He went out on his own, or he was persuaded by someone to go out in a nonviolent fashion."

"At the point of a gun is not nonviolent," I said.

"That's only a supposition, Mr. Haskell. We have no way of knowing that's so. How big a ransom would you say kidnappers might ask, Miss Ruysdale?"

"Mr. Chambrun is moderately well off," Ruysdale said, "but the owners could go very high."

"And would they?"

"I think," Ruysdale said, "Mr. Chambrun is more valuable to their investment than the real estate."

"Mr. Garrity assures me they've received no demand of any kind," Lewis said.

Ruysdale and I looked at each other, helplessly. No one had received any demands.

"One last thing," Lewis said. "There's a private elevator leading up to the penthouse?"

"It's one of a regular bank of elevators that goes to that wing of the hotel," I said, "but it is only used by Chambrun, or one of us going to the penthouse to see him for some reason."

" 'One of us'?"

"Miss Ruysdale, Jerry Dodd, the security chief, and sometimes I use it if the boss sends for me."

"If Chambrun wanted to leave the hotel, unseen, he could take that elevator down to the basement, couldn't he?" Lewis asked. "There must be ways of getting out to the street without encountering anyone, if you know your way around."

"The boss certainly knows his way around," I said.

"That elevator, according to Hardy," Lewis said, "was found at the penthouse level. Suggesting that he didn't use it to go down."

"It would be simple enough for someone to make it look that way," I said. "You ride the car down to the basement. When the doors open, you press the penthouse button, holding the doors open, and step out. The doors close, the car shoots up to the roof again. I've done it many times, not necessarily from the basement, you understand. I'd go to see the boss, he'd send me to see someone on one of the lower floors. I'd use the private elevator, go down to the tenth floor, say, and do what I told you; send the car back up to the penthouse so it would be there when the boss wanted it."

"So the elevator tells us nothing," Lewis said.

"I don't see that it does," I said.

Lewis shook his head. "There's been an all points bulletin out on him since early this morning," he said. "He's not a movie star, but thousands of people must know him by sight. Thirty years of traffic in and out of this hotel. Not a word from anywhere that anyone has seen him."

"He isn't circulating where anyone would see him," Ruysdale said, "or he would have been in touch long ago."

Lewis nodded. "I don't like to be a purveyor of gloom," he said, "but there is nothing about this so far that suggests a classic kidnapping-for-ransom. An enemy? A revenge for something? Some kind of nut? A discontented dishwasher?" When neither of us commented he said: "You seem to have had enough violence here today to last for a lifetime."

It looked as if there were a million dollars worth of flowers in the main ballroom. As I've said, the women looked spectacular. Shirley and I danced a little, but we weren't enjoying it as much as we should. People kept stopping us to ask me questions about the murder. A little before midnight the drummer in the band that was playing gave with a long roll that presaged an announcement.

Ont onto the bandstand came Claude Duval, his bald head glittering in the light from the crystal chandeliers. He was wearing a turtle-neck shirt, a gaudy plaid sports jacket, and black glasses. This was in marked contrast to the black and white ties, the evening gowns and jewels. Before he could speak, his name went around the room like a grass fire, and people started to applaud. Finally they were willing to listen.

"Ladies and gentlemen," he said, "I'm sure that most of you know that your ball committee and the hotel management have graciously permitted me to shoot a portion of my new film here tonight."

Applause.

"Janet Parker and Robert Randle will join the dancers on the floor followed by a movie camera. It is my hope that all of you will keep dancing, as though nothing unusual was happening. It will only interrupt your pleasure for ten or twelve minutes. In that time there will be unusually bright lights focused on the actors and on those of you on the fringe of the action. I hope you will not look startled or blink your eyes. In a few months you may be seen on screens all over the United States and Europe." He laughed. "I'm sure you wouldn't enjoy seeing yourselves making funny faces. Thank you for your indulgence and for taking part in this adventure." More applause. He evidently had something more to say. "I'm happy to tell you that the producer of my film *Strategies* is making a very generous contribution to the Cancer Fund as a way of expressing his thanks to you."

They handled it very well. The band began to play again, and after two or three minutes, the rubber-tired camera moved out onto the floor. Blinding lights focused on an area around it, and into that light came Janet Parker and Randle, dancing together. I hadn't been aware that they'd put in an appearance until they danced into camera range. A murmur of delight swept the room and the dancing couples crowded in on them.

Duval's voice came over some kind of loud speaker. "Please, ladies and gentlemen. Please! Don't focus your attention so noticeably on the actors. They are just another couple at a ball. We will stop the music for just a moment and then start again."

The music stopped. Makeup people rushed onto the floor to be certain the actors were okay. I saw a man blot at perspiration on Robert Randle's face with tissues. The lovely Janet Parker nodded and smiled at someone she knew, and then she caught sight of me. She smiled and her lips moved. I couldn't hear what she said but she made it quite clear. "Thanks!"

I hadn't done anything for her. If she was thanking me for keeping Mayberry out of her hair, her thanks belonged to Chambrun, one of his last acts before he disappeared.

The music started again and Shirley and I danced, self-consciously avoiding any interest in the two actors in the camera's eye. Eventually the music stopped and the dancers applauded the music as they would in a normal break. The two actors slipped away, surrounded by film people, and this time the applause was louder and for them. Garrity had been right. The ball guests had been delighted with the diversion.

Half an hour later Janet Parker and Randle were seated at a table in the Trapeze Bar which is located on the mezzanine above the lobby. Everybody in New York seemed to be trying to crowd into the bar which wouldn't hold over a hundred people seated at tables. Some of Jerry's people, pulled off the search for Chambrun, had to, physically, bar people from forcing their way in. This scene took longer to shoot, because it involved dialogue between the actors. In addition to the cameras were microphones, hung from a boom located over their heads. Duval was very much involved in this. He talked with the actors, backed off, signaled to the camera and light people. The actors would begin the scene, which was inaudible to Shirley and me, located at the far end of the room. Duval would rush forward, waving his arms. There was something wrong with the take. More talk to the actors and the camera man, more refreshing of makeup by the experts. There were at least ten takes before Duval, now the star of the evening from the onlookers' point of view, was finally satisfied.

I remember glancing at my watch. It was after two A.M. Chambrun had now been missing for twenty-four hours.

Shirley and I drifted away toward my apartment. It was not a night for love. Shirley understood that lovemaking, even sleep, were not in the cards for me.

"I'd like to stay in your apartment in case you need me," she said. "I brought a change of clothes when I thought something else was on the schedule."

"It would be nice to know you're here," I said.

Ruysdale was on my mind. She was living in a private hell, I knew. I changed out of my evening clothes into a sports jacket and slacks, kissed Shirley, and went off down the hall to Chambrun's office.

Ruysdale was there as I knew she would be. I was shocked by her appearance. She looked like a ghost of herself. She was sitting at Chambrun's desk, the telephone only inches away.

"In case he calls," she said, and I knew she no longer believed it was going to happen.

"You've got to get some rest," I said. I tried to make it sound light. "There's another day coming and we have a hotel to run."

It was the wrong note for her. That was always Chambrun's phrase in times of trouble—"a hotel to run." Tears welled up into her eyes.

"The filming went well," I told her. "I think Garrity was right. It took people's minds off the Kauffman thing."

"Hardy has nothing," she said in a dull voice. "He's traced down people who called Laura Kauffman during the evening, three or four who went to Twenty-one C to see her. All business about the ball. There were calls from outside he isn't able to check. Mayberry went to see her, but we know that. He went to try to get her help in persuading Pierre to change his mind about the filming. Duval talked to her on the phone, same objective. Mayberry, who saw her, says she was fine, everything perfectly normal. Duval says she sounded undisturbed. He had never met her or seen her, only the phone call, so his testimony doesn't mean much. There's a gap between the time Mayberry left her and found Pierre waiting in the hall, and an hour and a half later when Jim Kauffman found her. No one appears to have talked to her in that time. No phone calls. Elevator operators don't remember anyone unusual going to twenty-one. One of them remembered taking Jim Kauffman up, at about twenty to one. By the time Kauffman left two of the elevators were on self-service. He got one of those when he left. Whoever got to Laura managed it without attracting any attention."

"Coming or going," I said.

Ruysdale nodded. She covered her haggard face with hands that shook.

"You've got to get some rest," I said. "I'll stay here by the phone."

"Perhaps the couch," she said. "If you'll stay—"

Chambrun has a dressing room and bath that opens off the office. I went there and found a topcoat hanging in his closet. I brought it back, persuaded Ruysdale to lie down on the couch, and covered her with it. Then I took up the post at the desk, the telephone at my elbow.

I watched Ruysdale and, after a few restless moments, mercifully, she slept.

I slept too, after a while, my face buried on my arms on the desk. We'd all had just a little more than we could take. I was awakened by Ruysdale pushing me roughly away from the phone. There is no bell, only a little red light that blinks. She had seen it in her sleep.

"Miss Ruysdale speaking," she said. And then she cried out in a loud voice. "Pierre!"

I had the brains to switch on the squawk box on the desk so that I could hear the conversation.

"Ruysdale, listen to me very carefully," Chambrun said, his voice cold and flat.

"Pierre, are you all right? Where are you?"

"Listen to me, Ruysdale. There's no time for explanations. Are you listening?"

"Yes, Mr. Chambrun." She was suddenly the efficient secretary. "Mark is here with me, listening on the squawk box."

"In my penthouse there is the wall safe," Chambrun said. "You have the combination to it."

"Yes."

"Now listen carefully," Chambrun said. "In that safe is a time bomb, set to go off at nine o'clock."

I glanced at my wrist watch. It was a few minutes after eight. We had slept for about four hours, for God sake. Sunlight was pouring through the office windows.

"You are to call the bomb squad. Tell them they have less than an hour. You're not to do anything yourself, Ruysdale. You could blow yourself and the top of the hotel to pieces."

"Pierre! Where are you?"

"Somewhere in the wilds of New Jersey," Chambrun said. "No chance for me to get there. Now, move, Ruysdale!"

"Pierre, *are you all right?*"

"That is a laughable question," Chambrun said, and hung up.

PART 2

ONE

A hotel, run with Chambrun's kind of expertise, is prepared for any kind of contingency. Bomb threats, in recent years, are commonplace. Many of the best hotels in New York, including the Beaumont, have received them. So it was that while I, quite literally, froze at the message Chambrun had given us, Ruysdale was already dialing a number on the outside line. A list of special emergency numbers was carefully typed and pasted inside Chambrun's private book of numbers. There were, I knew, similar numbers at Ruysdale's desk, in the security office, at the front desk, and God knows where else. A number for the bomb squad—and a name to ask for—was on the list.

Ruysdale brought me to by pointing at the house phone. "Get Jerry Dodd here on the double," she said.

She was already talking to the bomb people when I located Jerry, told him we'd heard from Chambrun, and that we had big trouble.

"Where is he? Is he all right?" Jerry asked.

"No time to talk, pal," I said. "He's okay, I think. Alert as many men as you have on duty. We're going to need them."

"What the hell are you talking about?"

"Bomb," I said, and put down the phone.

Ruysdale had carried out her end of it. "It will take them ten or twelve minutes to get a squad here," she said. I looked at my watch. It was fourteen after eight. That would leave the bomb boys only a little more than half an hour to get the safe open and remove the explosive that could do who knows how much damage, cost how many lives!

"We are to evacuate the penthouses on the roof and the two floors below it," Ruysdale said.

There are three penthouses, including Chambrun's, on the roof. The two floors below had twenty-four suites each. There were probably something like a hundred and fifty people, including maids and staff, in the danger area. Panic, I thought.

We had one break. Just behind Jerry, as he came bursting into the office, was Lieutenant Hardy. The big policeman turned out to be a calm rock. He kept us on an even keel in those first minutes. Two elevators were to be isolated and kept in readiness for the bomb squad boys when they arrived. Security people, maids, a group of bellhops under Johnny Thacker, the day bell captain, were to go from penthouse to penthouse, room to room on the floors below and get people out. They weren't to stop to dress or collect belongings. Ruysdale pointed out that four floors down from the roof was the hotel's health club and gymnasium. It was a nonpublic place for the refugees to gather.

The whole process was underway within seven or eight minutes. In the midst of this organized confusion questions were fired.

"Did Chambrun say where he was?"

"Somewhere in New Jersey. No way for him to get here by nine."

"Did he say what happened to him?"

"He just said to hurry."

Hardy faced Ruysdale. "You do have the combination to the wall safe?"

She nodded.

"Then you wait at the lobby level for the bomb squad people."

"What about the phones—in case he calls again?" she asked.

"You, Mark," Hardy said to me. "Use the house phone to alert everyone on the staff. They have to know, but they have to keep it to themselves or the hotel will turn into a madhouse."

"You think only those two floors below the roof are in danger?" I asked him.

"You can't put an atom bomb in a wall safe," Hardy said. "But it could be powerful enough to rip off quite a little real estate. Let's stop talking and get to it!" He gave me a wry smile. "Chambrun did sound okay?"

"He sounded like himself," I said.

Everyone who works in the Beaumont has been chosen with care. As I spread the word through the switchboard and the daytime chief operator, Mrs. Veach, there wasn't the faintest hint of hysteria.

"Should I notify Doc Partridge and the infirmary staff?" Mrs. Veach asked. "If people should be hurt, police or guests—?"

"Good girl," I said.

When I had covered everything I called my apartment. While I waited for Shirley to answer I heard the police sirens down at the street level. It was twenty-eight minutes after eight; thirty-two minutes to go. Shirley didn't answer. I guessed she was old-fashioned enough to think it wouldn't be proper for a woman to pick up the phone in my rooms. I rang again—and a third time. Maybe she'd get the idea. She did.

"Are you up and dressed?" I asked her.

"Well—" She sounded sleepy.

"There's a bomb threat," I said. "It's on the roof, so we're fairly safe down here. But I'd feel better if you'd join me in Chambrun's office so I'd know where you are."

"Bomb?"

"Chambrun phoned in the warning. He seems to be in one piece."

"Oh, I'm glad, Mark. Five minutes."

People, as a whole, are really amazing in crisis. Perhaps it's because, in this day and age, we have schooled ourselves to expect the unexpected. It must cross people's minds, when they board a jet liner for London, they might just wind up in Lebanon. If it happens, they are curiously prepared. An old lady who takes her poodle out for a last walk at night knows it's possible some goons may clobber her and steal her purse. Older citizens know that when they return from the supermarket with the day's groceries someone may push them into their apartments and rob them. Violence is not unexpected, but very few people change their plans or their routines. I learned afterwards that not one of the people on those upper floors, guests and staff, resisted for a moment being herded down into the health club. Buildings were constantly being evacuated after bomb threats in today's city. What a world!

Shirley could wake up in the middle of a desert sandstorm and look lovely. How she did it in five minutes I can't tell you. She came quickly across the office and I held her very close for a moment. Life felt

real again and not like the science-fiction nightmare
of the last half hour. I brought her up to date.

"Mr. Chambrun didn't tell you what had happened
to him?"

"No, just what was cooking. He sounded as though
we could expect him to turn up, but not in time for
whatever."

"What can I do?" she asked.

"Just stay here so I can keep reminding myself that
there is something worth sticking around for." I kissed
the tip of her upturned nose. "You ever made Turkish
coffee?" I asked. "There's the special coffee maker
over there."

"I guess I could figure it out," she said.

"Ruysdale didn't get to it," I said. "If Chambrun
gets back here and there's no Turkish coffee—after a
day and a half—!"

Secondhand, I can tell you a little of something that
was going on elsewhere. The lobby traffic was only
mildly disturbed, I was told, when the bomb squad
people arrived, dressed like men from Mars and carrying some sort of metal pot between them. The word
had been so tightly kept that I imagine people
thought this was a new laundry service dressed in
some kind of mod uniforms. The penthouses and the
two top floors were deserted, the evacuation smoothly
accomplished by Hardy and Jerry Dodd. It was Jerry
who took the bomb squad people, equipped now with
Ruysdale's safe combination, to Chambrun's quarters
and showed them the wall safe, hidden behind a colorful Gauguin painting. Jerry told me that the man in
charge produced something that looked like a stetho-
scope and held it against the safe's dial.

"Ticking away," the man said, and glanced at his watch. Twenty-three minutes to go.

Then everyone except the experts were cleared out of the penthouse and told to go at least three floors down.

In Chamburn's office Shirley and I waited. Ten minutes to nine—five minutes to nine—three minutes to nine. Nine o'clock. We strained to hear some sound, clinging to each other. Nothing. About five minutes past nine Ruysdale and Lieutenant Hardy walked into the office. I couldn't read their faces.

"I know how lousy that Turkish coffee is," Hardy said, "but I think I could stand a cup of it."

"They made it?" I asked, as Shirley went to get him his coffee.

"They made it," Hardy said.

Ruysdale started to laugh, a little hysterically for her.

"An alarm clock," Hardy said. "An ordinary, drugstore alarm clock."

"Attached to—?" I asked.

"Nothing," Hardy said.

"What are you talking about?"

"It was attached to nothing," Hardy said. "No explosives, no nothing. Just ticking its little heart away inside the safe."

"A hoax!" I said, not really believing it.

"A hoax," Hardy said. "A good enough one to have convinced Chambrun, it seems. Now all we can do is wait for him to explain it."

I can't tell you too much about the general activity in the hotel for the next hour. I know that the evacuated guests were returned to their rooms. There was no longer any danger. That made it all a kind of a lark to them; something to dine out on for the next month. Chambrun's office, where I stayed, became a madhouse of people coming and going. I got to Mrs. Veach on the switchboard and told her to spread the word that we had an all-clear. Jerry Dodd and several of his security men, Atterbury from the front desk, the chief engineer, strangers I'd never seen before, were all asking questions for which there were no answers.

Some facts emerged from Sergeant Bragiotti of the bomb squad, a dark-skinned, burly man who had learned to live with moments of high tension. Through it all the phones kept ringing and Ruysdale was busy reassuring guests that there was no danger. There had been no way to keep a hundred and fifty evacuees from spreading the word. False alarm was the message Ruysdale was handing out, and she had pressed Shirley into handling one of the phones.

Bragiotti, still wearing some sort of fireproof coverall and carrying a heavy metal helmet with a glass face shield, repeated the unbelievable news.

"A forty-eight-hour clock," he told us. "You can find one in almost any drugstore. It was set to go off at nine this morning. But nothing else; no explosives, no gadgets, nothing."

"What would have happened when the alarm rang?" someone asked.

"Nothing," Bragiotti said. "If you were standing close enough to the safe you might have heard the bell. That's all."

"Chambrun thought it was real," I said.

"So did I," Bragiotti said, "when I first heard the ticking sound. An ordinary clock can be used to trigger a bomb."

"How the hell did someone get the clock into the safe," Jerry Dodd asked.

"Opened it, put it in," Bragiotti said.

"Only Miss Ruysdale and Chambrun have the combination," Jerry said.

Bragiotti shrugged, glancing across the office at Ruysdale who was busy on one of the phones.

"You know damn well neither one of them did it!" Jerry said.

Bragiotti found a cigarette somewhere inside his asbestos suit. "That safe is probably twenty-five or thirty years old," he said. "It's what, in my business, we call a Jimmy Valentine. Anyone with any skill could have opened it without the combination. I could have opened it without the combination if Miss Ruysdale hadn't had it. Piece of cake. You just listen to the tumblers drop and you've got it."

"But you'd have to know how?" Jerry said.

"It's almost a lost art," Bragiotti said, "because they don't make locks that simple these days. But it could have been done. Must have been done because the safe wasn't forced."

"Fingerprints?" Jerry asked.

"Wiped clean," Bragiotti said.

"Can the clock be traced?"

"No prints on the clock, also wiped clean," Bragiotti said. "Could have been bought anywhere between here and San Francisco. You could try for months and not come up with an answer."

"The whole damn thing is some kind of joke!" Jerry said.

"Not such a funny joke." It was Frank Lewis, the FBI man, who had come in without my noticing him. "If someone took Chambrun by force out into New

Jersey somewhere, it's kidnapping. Across state lines. That's not a joke when we catch him."

"You know he was taken away from here against his will?" Bragiotti asked.

"No other way," Jerry said. "If you knew the man, you'd know."

"There's nothing more I can do for you, or tell you," Bragiotti said. He hesitated. "Chambrun did tell you on the phone that the bomb was in the safe? Not just a bomb somewhere?"

"He told us in the safe," I said. "He mentioned the fact that Ruysdale had the combination."

"It might make sense to search the whole hotel," Bragiotti said. "But if he was so positive—and the clock *was* there—"

"What's this about a clock?"

And there he was, standing inside the office door. Chambrun! His gray tropical worsted suit looked as though he'd slept in it, and it turned out he had.

Ruysdale almost blew her own secret then, if she had one. She bolted from the telephone and ran across the room to him. I thought she was going to embrace him.

"I'm all right, Ruysdale," he said, gently for him. It stopped her.

We all crowded around him, all asking silly questions. He walked past us to his desk and sat down. At last God *was* in his heaven. He gestured toward the Turkish coffee maker. Ruysdale reached it first and brought him a cup. He tasted it.

"My God, who made this?" he asked.

"I—I'm afraid I did, Mr. Chambrun," Shirley said.

"You need schooling," he said. He leaned back in

his chair, lighting one of his Egyptian cigarettes. "The bomb?"

Bragiotti filled him in on our end of the story. The bomb was a hoax. Chambrun's next question was how the guests had been handled and what their reactions had been. He seemed satisfied with the answers.

"So you'd better hear my end of it," he said.

He had gone to his penthouse at one fifteen in the morning, as we knew from the phone logs. He had put some music on his stereo, gone out onto the roof garden for a few minutes, a standard relaxing routine on a fair night. He had come back into the penthouse and sat down to make some notes for the next day's activities. At two fifteen he'd checked with the switchboard, as we knew. No more calls except in an emergency.

"I turned to go into the bedroom," he told us, "and found myself facing a small, wiry man wearing a ski mask and holding a very large handgun pointed at me. A .44 caliber cannon, I think. How he got there I have no idea. The gun was very real."

The masked man told Chambrun he was going to have to leave the hotel. If he went, without making trouble, he wouldn't be hurt. If he was forced to use the gun on Chambrun that would only be the beginning.

"He told me there was a bomb in the safe, set to go off at nine o'clock this morning. That was some thirty and a half hours away. I didn't believe him. He suggested I go over to the safe and listen. I put my ear against the dial and I could her the timing mechanism ticking away. He wasn't kidding, I thought."

The hotel was more important to Chambrun than

his own safety. He might, he told us, have made some attempt to disarm the masked man. Long ago, in the days of the Resistance, he had learned how to handle himself. But it was no better than a fifty-fifty chance. If he failed he could wind up dead. No one would have had any reason to look in the safe. There was nothing of any real importance kept there. He would be dead, and at nine o'clock this morning the top of the hotel could be blown to pieces and who knows how many people killed and injured.

"He told me that if I played the game his way I would be set free in time to have the bomb deactivated," Chambrun said. "I asked him what it was all about. He wasn't talking. Somehow he convinced me he was dead serious. A harmless alarm clock, for God sake!"

The blessed hotel had to be protected. Chambrun, gun at his back, took the masked man down to the basement in the private elevator. They sent the car back up to the roof, just the way I'd suggested to Hardy. Chambrun led the man out onto the side street where there was a car waiting. Chambrun was forced to drive.

"So you know where you went?" the FBI man asked.

"Of course I know where I went," Chambrun said. "At least most of the way. This morning I know exactly where I was."

"Where?" the FBI man asked.

"About twenty miles south of Princeton, New Jersey. We went out through the Holland Tunnel, up over the Pulaski Skyway, and on to Princeton. All familiar. But then he took me onto back roads. In the dark it was hard to pick out landmarks. It doesn't matter because this morning I know. I can send you to the cottage where I was held."

"He had a gun on you all this time?"

Chambrun made an impatient gesture. "We got to a simple little summer cottage. There was early daylight then. He never left me for an instant. About eight o'clock in the morning he asked me if I'd like some coffee. I would. There was some made in a pot on the stove. He told me to heat it up. I did, poured two cups. He wouldn't let me get close enough to him to hand him his cup. He must have read my mind. I thought of throwing the hot coffee in his face and trying to jump him. I needed the coffee. I took a couple of deep swallows of it. It was the worst coffee I ever tasted." He glanced at Shirley. "You are a genius compared to whoever made that stuff, Miss Thomas. After a moment I understood why it was so awful. The room began to spin around, and that sonofabitch in the mask was laughing at me. It was drugged. I fell flat on my face on the floor." Chambrun's face was set in rock-hard lines. "When I came to I couldn't move, my muscles were so cramped. I looked at my watch. It was a few minutes past eight. I thought I'd only been out for a few minutes. Then I saw the calendar on the watch face. I'd been out for nearly twenty-four hours! And there was a bomb set to go off in less than an hour.

"No sign of my masked friend. I struggled up, holding onto a chair to steady myself. There was a telephone on a side table. To my surprise it worked. I called you, Ruysdale. I prayed a little that I was in time. A harmless alarm clock! It doesn't make sense."

"How did you get back here?" Lewis asked.

"The car we'd come in was gone," Chambrun said.

"I followed a country road till I came to a house. A man there drove me into Princeton where I hired a car."

"Draw me a map so I can locate the cottage," Lewis said. "Your friend must have left his fingerprints there."

Chambrun picked up a pencil and began to draw. "I never saw him without gloves," he said.

To quote from an oft quoted quote, there was a hotel to run. Frank Lewis, the FBI man, took off for New Jersey and the cottage where Chambrun had been an unconscious prisoner. Bragiotti went back to his headquarters to wait for another bomb scare from somewhere. They came every day, he told us. Shirley, without a word but with a signal to me, slipped away. She'd be in my apartment when I was free. I supposed that my job would be to circulate in the lobby and the other public rooms, to answer questions, to satisfy guests that there was no longer any danger or threat of danger.

I was just about to take off when I got a look from Chambrun which told me to wait. He then turned to Hardy who was standing by the windows overlooking the park.

"Nice of you to help, Walter," Chambrun said. "A friend is a friend is a friend."

"I'm not here as a friend," Hardy said.

"Oh?"

"You've got a murder on your hands, Pierre," the big detective said.

I suddenly realized that Chambrun didn't know about anything that had happened in the Beaumont for nearly thirty-six hours. In his hurry to get back

from New Jersey he hadn't stopped to buy a paper. If there had been a radio in his hired car, he obviously hadn't turned it on. Chambrun looked
stunned.

In a casual, conversational tone Hardy gave him the
details of Laura Kauffman's slaughter. He didn't leave
out any of the gory details. As I listened to them
again, I was glad I hadn't bothered with breakfast.
When Hardy was finished, Chambrun turned to me.

"Reaction in the hotel?" he asked.

"What you might expect," I said. "She was chairman
of the Cancer Fund Ball committee. No way to keep it
a secret from her committee people. Thousands of
people were suddenly asking questions. We had no answers for them."

"We still have no answers," Hardy said.

"The ball went on, however?"

I swallowed hard. "Yes, but with a few changes in
the schedule." I told him that we had given in to Duval's demands. I gave him Garrity's reasons for giving
in, and admitted to having been sold. "It worked,
boss," I said. "Most of the guests forgot about the
murder and drooled over the stars and the genius-
director."

Chambrun's eyes were cold. "We'll have to talk
about that later," he said. Then back to Hardy. "No
leads?"

"The woman's husband. He's under arrest, but here
in your infirmary. A first-class case of delirium tre-
mens."

Hardy then went over the facts as we knew them.
Laura had been alive, we assumed, when Mayberry
went to visit her shortly after ten.

"You picked up Mayberry as he was leaving her

suite," Hardy said. "You'd been visiting Janet Parker. Mayberry tells us Mrs. Kauffman was fine when he left her. The husband came here about twenty minutes to one and found her dead."

"But I was here, in the Spartan Bar at that time," Chambrun said.

"Kauffman didn't report what he'd found. He just grabbed a bottle of booze and high-tailed it out of here," Hardy said. "No one reported Mrs. Kauffman's death until the security people went into her suite looking for you sometime after breakfast yesterday morning."

"Does the medical examiner say when she died?"

"Sometime between ten and twelve the night before. We know she was alive about eleven, the time when Mayberry left her and met you in the hall. That seems to narrow the time to between eleven and twelve, give or take something on the long end."

"Give two hours so that the husband could have done it?" Chambrun asked.

"Time of death is not something you can ever pinpoint," Hardy said. "In detective stories somebody breaks a watch, or shoots a hole in a clock—"

"Don't mention clocks," Chambrun said.

"In real life," Hardy said, "there are other factors; room temperatures, condition of the body, other details. It's never more than an educated guess. I suppose the M.E. could be two hours off."

"You buy the husband?"

Hardy shrugged. "It would make it easy," he said. "This woman had a history of rather scandalous involvements with a great many men. With the help of Miss Thomas we're trying to compile a list of possibles. We have no real evidence against James Kauffman. He came in on his own—with a little nudging from Miss Thomas. He admitted to being here, finding his wife dead. He admitted to running out. You play hunches, Pierre. I have a hunch James Kauffman is clean."

"But you're holding him?"

"When he's got a grip on himself he can probably tell us more about Mrs. Kauffman's involvements than anyone."

Chambrun lit a fresh cigarette, his eyes almost buried in their deep pouches. "I can tell you something about early involvements," he said. "I knew her when she was eighteen years old. That goes back thirty-five years."

"You knew her personally then?" Hardy asked.

"Yes."

"But that was during World War Two. You were in the French Resistance then, weren't you?"

"That's where I knew her. In Paris," Chambrun said. His mouth tightened. "Occupied Paris. She was Laura Hemmerly then. She'd already been married once, but she took back her maiden name after an annulment arranged by her father. Jason Hemmerly, big operator in steel."

"We know some of this, boss," I said. "A ski instructor was the first husband. But Shirley has it that the Hemmerlys hurried back home when France wasn't safe for them anymore."

"Shirley has it wrong," Chambrun said. His voice sounded flat as though it pained him to remember. "Laura Hemmerly did not go back to America with her father. She stayed in Paris, in a little apartment on the Avenue Klebert. That's where the action was, the greatest action in history. The occupation of the world's most beautiful city by the bastards of all time."

He paused a minute, picked up the cold coffee, tasted it and made a wry face. Both Hardy and I realized this wasn't the moment to press him to go on.

"I was fighting underground for France in those days. I was as American as you are, graduated from Cornell. I was twenty-three. American citizen. But France was in my blood. It was where I had to be at that point in time. In some respects, in spite of the grim realities around me, a city and its people under the heel of a tyrant, I was naive. I thought all Americans could be trusted. I thought all Americans must feel about the Nazis the way I did." His smile was bitter. "It nearly cost me my life. And that bitch in your morgue, Walter, was responsible. She has denied it always, but I have never had any doubts." He glanced at Ruysdale. "Could you possibly make me some decent coffee, Betsy?" It was the first time I'd ever heard him call her by her first name.

Ruysdale went to the sideboard. Hardy and I waited for him again. A man was dredging up things that hurt him deeply. You couldn't rush him.

"In the underground," he said finally, "we had a target. He was a man named Hugo Perrault. They called him the Butcher of Montmartre. He was a collaborator of the first order. He turned over hundreds, maybe thousands of people to the Gestapo. He headed execution squads himself. He was a monster. They said, when the war was over and the Germans had won it, he would be the tyrant of Paris. He would go on butchering anyone who had sided against the Nazis. We wanted him, wanted him badly. And I, God help me, was so clever!" He drew a deep breath.

"There was Laura Hemmerly, eighteen, American, so brave I thought. And so lovely to look at. She had stayed in France, with the French people she loved who were in such dire straights, rather than go safely home with her father. A heroine." He gave us that twisted, bitter little smile again. "At twenty-three I believed in heroines, and heroes. God knows, there were heroes all around me. And there was Laura Hemmerly who had to be a heroine. You understand, in Paris, in those black days, if you lived out in the open you had to play ball with the conquerors. A rich American girl who had chosen to stay in Paris? Those maniacs assumed she must sympathize with the conquerors. Nazi officers in command of the occupation beat a path to her door, as the saying goes. I, with only one purpose in life, supposed that Laura Hemmerly only played the the social game with them because she had to. I supposed that she, a lovely American girl, would do anything she could to strike a blow against them." Chambrun shook his head. "I was told later—there was a joke in the underground—that she had to have sex every four hours or she developed severe migraine headaches. She couldn't stand the pain, so—"

"Every four hours!" I heard myself say.

"Probably an exaggeration," Chambrun said. "More likely every eight hours. But I hadn't heard that then. I managed to meet her—my little American heroine. I suggested that through her Nazi acquaintances she might be able to find out where Hugo Perrault holed up, where we could find him in an off-guard moment. She was wide-eyed, eager to help the brave Resistance. If I would come to her apartment three nights from then, she might have information for me.

"My friends warned against it. Whatever her sympathies she would be too frightened of her Nazi friends to work against them. Naive, I said I was. She was American. She loved the French people and France, where she had spent so much of her childhood. I kept my appointment with her.

"She received me in her charming little Avenue Klebert apartment. She was wearing some sort of transparent negligee. I know now that she was prepared for lovemaking, but I was not. What had she learned? Where could we find the Butcher of Montmartre? She began to give me some vague bits and pieces. This officer had told her one thing, this one another. This was likely, that was not likely. I should have recognized a stall, a betrayal, but I didn't. She was a fine, decent American girl. Suddenly the door to the apartment burst open and there, facing me, was Hugo Perrault, the Butcher, armed with a submachine gun. He began screaming at me in French. I wanted to know where he was. Well, here he was! If I had prayers to say I must say them quickly.

"I remember glancing, reproachfully, at Laura. She was standing with her back to the wall, arms spread out, with a look of such intense excitement in her eyes I couldn't believe it. The prospect of seeing me murdered was providing her with an excitement beyond a sexual climax. She couldn't wait for it to happen. I swear she was screaming at Perrault, 'Now! Now!' "

Chambrun reached for the fresh coffee Ruysdale brought him. He took a sip and let his breath out in a little sigh of pleasure.

"I was standing by a little straight-backed chair," he said. "I wasn't naive any longer. I threw the chair at Perrault and made a dive at the window. He started firing his gun, but he'd been knocked off balance. I went through the window, glass, frame and all. It was two stories down to the courtyard. My ankle was hurt, my left wrist was broken, but I managed to scramble away. Perrault was firing at me from the smashed window, but by some miracle I got free. Two completely innocent pedestrains were shot to death in the street behind me." He took another sip of coffee and put down his cup. "I told you I could tell you about early involvements," he said very quietly. "That was Laura Hemmerly at eighteen—thirty-five years ago."

Hardy spoke after a moment. "From the looks of her when we found her it could be her butcher friend caught up with her."

Chambrun shook his head. "Perrault died less than two years after the incident I've described. The Allies were entering Paris. Perrault was at the top of their war criminals list. He tried to escape in a small private plane, and it crashed and burned."

Hardy sighed. "So we are not looking for Hugo Perrault."

"But you know something about the woman," Chambrun said. "Treachery, betrayal, violence were like sexual delights to her."

"She married a German," I said. "The Baron von Holtzmann."

"An interesting and very courageous man," Chambrun said. "I knew him well. He collaborated with the Resistance. He hated Hitler and his people as much as we did. He played both sides of the street, dangerously, skillfully. But he was one of us."

"He committed suicide after five years of marriage. Why?" I asked.

"I can only guess," Chambrun said. "I had lost track

of him. I was back here, running this hotel, when he blew his brains out. I think he must have learned that the woman in his bed had spent the war frolicking with Nazi pigs. He couldn't stand the thought of it." Chambrun lit a fresh cigarette. "Pick up the trail after that suicide, Walter, and it may lead you to your murderer."

"Something I don't understand," I said.

"Yes, Mark?"

"She came here, engaged a suite, chairman of the Cancer Fund Ball committee. You knew all this about her and you didn't interfere. You let her be here as a guest."

Chambrun leaned back in his chair, eyelids lowered. "What I've told you took place thirty-five years ago. Values, during the occupation, were, to put it mildly, different. You think of me as a civilized, sophisticated, decent sort of human being, no?"

"Yes," I said.

"Well, thirty-five years ago I killed men, with a gun, with a knife, with my bare hands. I understand the excesses that all men—and women—may have been driven to in those evil times. Laura Hemmerly—Laura von Holtzman—Laura Kauffman; a whore for the Nazis in one period of her life, the wife of a hero in another, and an international hostess and person of great charm in a third, and then she takes a young lover, James Kauffman, as she approaches middle age, and eventually marries him. She is at the center of important and worthwhile charities. What happens if I bar her from the hotel for what she did to me in hysterical times?"

"Did you meet her here?" Hardy asked. "Did you discuss that past with her?"

Chambrun smiled at him. He touched his face with his finger tips, and then spread his hands over his plumpish midsection. "Do I look like a man who would jump out a second-story window and land on his feet, like a swashbuckling Douglas Fairbanks, Senior? I was twenty-three years old then. None of us used our real names in the Resistance. Laura Kauffman came here about the ball. She sat in that chair where you're sitting, Hardy. We talked for half an hour about the plans for the ball, and there wasn't the slightest gleam of recognition. Either she was a great actress, or so many men have passed in and out of her life that thirty-five years ago was a blur. And, I have changed."

"You didn't want to punish her?"

"My dear Mark, if I had lived with hate all these years I would be dead of it."

"You think she didn't recognize you?" Hardy asked.

"Unless she was an actress beyond compare," Chambrun said.

TWO

The hotel lived and functioned at something like normal. People were curious about the murder, of course. Almost no one, except the staff, asked about Chambrun. He made a point of circulating. He had been absent for a day and a half which didn't seem abnormal to the guests. A man has business to transact that could take him away from his desk.

Below the surface two mysteries had us by the short hairs. The murder was in the competent hands of Lieutenant Hardy. What concerned Chambrun most was the reason for his abduction and the phony bomb. Who and why? Chambrun was intent on finding those answers for himself. Only Frank Lewis, the FBI man, who had gone out to New Jersey to examine the cottage where Chambrun had been held, seemed to be working on that problem.

About lunchtime Chambrun assembled Ruysdale, Jerry Dodd, George Atterbury, the front-desk man, and me in his office.

"The only possible reason for this charade," he said to us, "was to get me out of the hotel for thirty-odd hours. That has to mean that something went on here that I was not to see or hear about. Something that couldn't have happened if I'd been here to see and know about." He looked at us, eyebrows raised in question.

"The murder," Atterbury said. He is a plump little man with heavy, shell-rimmed glasses. He looks like an accountant, which is really what he is. Credit ratings are his specialty.

"The murder took place while I was still here and circulating," Chambrun said. "My presence didn't prevent it. Something else. Something was planned here that I mustn't see or be aware of. Yet everyone else was on the job. It apparently didn't matter if they saw what I was not allowed to see."

"Someone in the hotel that you wouldn't have wanted here," Atterbury suggested. He took some file cards out of his pocket. "You haven't been over the new registrations for the last two mornings, Mr. Chambrun."

I have mentioned this routine, the daily check on new guests with the special information on them, credit, habits, moral or immoral. And the cards initialed P.C., which meant Chambrun has special facts about them which he kept to himself. Atterbury suggested it could be one of those P.C. guests who didn't want Chambrun to know he was in the hotel.

"And risk a kidnapping charge just to keep me out of sight while he was here?" Chambrun shook his head. "But let's look at your cards, Atterbury."

The cards Chambrun should have seen the morning of his disappearance came first. Most of them were people with past records, people who had used the hotel, many of them many times before. There were the movie people. They had checked in the early afternoon of the day before. Their cards wouldn't have appeared on Chambrun's desk until the next morning.

Chambrun went over the names. There were Janet Parker, Robert Randle, the two stars. The only unusual information on them was the letter G on Randle's card which indicated certain sexual preferences. There were Clark Herman, Claude Duval, Jacques Bordeau, Chester Cole, and a dozen technicians and cameramen. Chambrun knew all the principals by sight and by reputation.

"Except Jacques Bordeau," he said. "Who is he?"

"Duval's secretary," Atterbury said.

I remembered the mousy little man who had held an ashtray for Duval during my interview with the director. "Young fellow in his middle twenties," I said. "Mr. Anonymous."

They all had unlimited credit. It went with the movie company.

"I'd like to have a look at all these people I don't know," Chambrun said. "The technicians and cameramen, and this Jacques Bordeau."

"Not possible," Atterbury said. "Duval and Bordeau checked out about five o'clock this morning, after the filming in the Trapeze. I understand they have a filming on the coast with other actors besides the stars today. The rest of them have checked out this morning, or are in the process of checking out."

Chambrun sat frowning at the cards. There was evidently nothing that caught his attention on those first cards or this morning's batch. He knew who almost all of them were, and the information on the ones he didn't know was satisfactory.

"There's still the chance you were gotten out of here so they could change the times for the filming," Jerry Dodd said. "Your orders were overridden, which is what they wanted."

"I just can't buy that," Chambrun said. "Risk a kidnapping charge just to get a camera on the dance floor? Risk the chance that I might have tangled with my masked friend and brought about a murder—just to get a camera on the dance floor? It doesn't add up, Jerry. Not to me."

"It could," I said, trying to be helpful, "have been just some sort of overdone practical joke. No bomb, really. Man in a ski mask is right out of television melodrama. He could have held you up with a toy gun. If you'd made a grab at him, he'd have torn off his mask and died laughing. Some crazy bastard who gets a kick out of making people look foolish."

Chambrun gave me a bored look. "That's nothing short of brilliant, Mark," he said, "except for one fact. It wasn't a toy gun. Take my word for it. I forgive you, though. Because my first thought, when that character appeared in the penthouse, was that it was some kind of joke. It was so far out I thought it couldn't be real. But I know guns. That was a genuine .44. No risks were too great for it to be anything short of vital to someone that I be out of the hotel for a stretch of time."

"It was so well prepared in advance," Jerry Dodd said. "He had to get into your penthouse. He had to get into the wall safe. From the way you told it, that drugged pot of coffee in the New Jersey cottage had to have been prepared well in advance. Something that could knock you out for twenty-four hours could have killed you."

"I'm a tough old bird," Chambrun said. "Let's talk about locks and safes."

"He got into your penthouse, which involves a lock. He got into your safe, not too difficult according to the bomb squad guy. Let's begin with the lock on the penthouse door. Hotel thieves know how to open locked doors. We face that problem all the time. He didn't have to steal a passkey from the maid service. If he could open a safe without the combination, he could probably open the lock on the door."

"A professional," Chambrun said.

"No doubt about that," Jerry said. "So having planted his clock in your safe, he probably stayed hidden in the penthouse, waiting for you to arrive, the sound of any manipulating of the door lock covered by the music you were playing on your stereo."

"And if he stayed hidden in the penthouse, waiting for me, why did he wait a whole hour until I made my goodnight call to the switchboard before he showed himself? If he was hidden there, he must have known I was going to make that call, which would shut me off from the outside."

"Knew your routines," Jerry said.

"Who knows them but you, and Mark, and Ruysdale, and the girls on the switchboard?" Chambrun asked.

"It isn't exactly a state secret," Jerry said. "Somebody could have mentioned it casually, gossiped about it. People are always curious about you, your eccentricities."

"I'm not so goddamned eccentric," Chambrun said.

"Fact of the matter is, though, this guy had to be well prepared in advance. Nothing spur-of-the-moment about it. He has a cottage in New Jersey, advance preparation. He has a drugged pot of coffee, advanced preparation. He knew how to get the door open, knew there was a safe, knew it was old-fashioned and that he could open it. Knew your phone routines. All that took some research. Who was he? Who gave him the facts he needed? And what good did it do him simply to have you absent for thirty hours? They could have asked for a ransom and gotten it, so money wasn't the object."

"You haven't even been up to the penthouse," I said. "How do we know he didn't steal something valuable? He needed time to get away with it."

"He didn't take anything with him—except me," Chambrun said. "There's nothing worth all that preparation and risk to steal except three paintings and a few curios. They were all in place when we left. I don't keep money there, I keep it in the bank!"

Ruysdale spoke for the first time. Chambrun's return had restored her to her cool, efficient self.

"A professional of that caliber suggests a man who could be hired by someone else," she said. "Maybe that's what we should be thinking about, the employer not the employee."

Chambrun gave her a rare smile. "Bless you, Ruysdale, for suggesting an obvious which I had overlooked," he said.

Jerry Dodd had another concern. "How safe are you now?" he asked Chambrun.

"I believe quite safe if you think of the facts," Chambrun said. "I was drugged and left alone in that Jersey cottage. No restraints on me; a working telephone there for me to use. I was free to go, free to spread any sort of alarms I chose. I was naturally concerned about the bomb which I thought was real. But whatever it was I wasn't supposed to see or know about has happened. I am, obviously, no longer a threat to them. But I want to tell you, Jerry, I am goddamned curious! What went on here in those thirty hours? What the hell went on here?"

I went up to the penthouse with Chambrun. The three penthouses on the roof of the Beaumont are co-ops, owned by the tenants, but serviced by the hotel. One was Chambrun's, one belonged to a delightful but slightly dotty old lady who looked like an old-time Helen Hokinson drawing, the third had been recently acquired by the new owners' group. It was used for special guests, parties, perhaps an overnight stop for one of the owners. Nobody was in permanent residence. I had checked and found that on the night of Chambrun's abduction that third penthouse had been occupied by a British industrialist named Jonathan Harkness. He had, in fact, been in residence for about a week and was still there. The facts on his registration card were impeccable: unlimited credit, a family man who had not brought his family with him, good connections with his own government and ours. He was a personal friend of Garrity's, our board chairman.

Only two elevators go to the roof. One of them is reserved strictly for Chambrun. Old Mrs. Victoria Haven and whoever is in Penthouse Three use the other one. Chambrun's elevator is self-service round the clock, the other is always run by an operator. I want to point out that while Chambrun's elevator is private, there is nothing to prevent someone who wants to break the rules from using it, if they chose to risk the wrath of God.

Chambrun's penthouse is the epitome of disorganized elegance. Nothing to steal but three paintings, he'd said, but those three paintings were a Gauguin, a

Matisse, and a Degas, probably worth a million bucks in cold cash. Over the years there had been gifts from all sorts of celebrated people for whom Chambrun had done favors. You had the feeling that everything in the place was loved and had a special significance for Chambrun. An interior decorator might have been outraged, but a visitor was instantly entranced by the awareness of a lived-in luxury.

One thing is certain. A professional thief would have found plenty of things worth stealing. Which made it clear that the "professional" in whom we were interested was not a professional thief. After a brief look around Chambrun announced there was nothing whatever missing.

"Things like this," he said, picking up a little silver snuffbox from a side table. "Given to me by a dethroned king, worth at least five thousand dollars. He could have slipped it in his pocket. He evidently wasn't interested."

Jerry Dodd has assured us that the lock on the door hadn't been forced, but Chambrun examined it himself. Not a scratch, not a mark of any sort.

There were the French doors leading out to Chambrun's private roof garden. I don't know when he found the time, but he enjoyed messing around with plants. Those French doors are not only fastened by conventional Yale locks, but there are iron bars inside that slide across and make them impenetrable. They were never left open or unlocked except when Chambrun went out to the garden. When he came back in they were relocked and barred. Routine from which he never varied.

"Did you go out to the roof when you came up from the Spartan Bar night before last?" I asked him.

"For a few minutes. It waas a beautiful night."

"He could have slipped in behind you without your noticing," I said.

"And then, when I came back in and was there, he opened the safe and put his clock in it? No, Mark. That had to be done before I ever came upstairs. It would take a little time, even for an expert, to open that safe."

"Unless he had the combination."

"Only Ruysdale and I had the combination," he said.

That was that.

If the kidnapper had come in earlier and hidden someplace, there was no sign of it.

"There are no hiding places that I didn't cover, not looking for anything, you understand. I changed clothes. I was wearing a dinner jacket when I went up there. So I went into my clothes closet. I went to the john, natural reasons. I went to the kitchen to make myself a drink. He couldn't have hidden in the broom closet. It's too small."

"The spare bedroom?" I asked.

"It just happens that the air-conditioning unit is located in the spare bedroom's closet," he said. "Inconvenient, but there it is. It was a warm night. I went in there to turn it on. He wasn't hiding here, Mark. As Jerry suggested, he must have come in the front door—a second time—any noise he made covered by the music I was playing. A Beethoven symphony."

"He must have scouted out the territory before he made his move," I said.

"So let's see if Victoria Haven or Jonathan Harkness saw anything," he said.

Victoria Haven is a kind of landmark at the Beaumont. She had bought the first co-op in the hotel nearly thirty years ago, just about the time Chambrun had taken over as manager. She broke all the rules, primarily the rule of keeping animals in the hotel. She had kept several generations of obnoxious little Japanese spaniels in her penthouse, and it would have taken the National Guard to get rid of any of them. Chambrun, who was ironfisted about rules, chose to go along with the old girl's foibles. She must be eighty now, I thought, which made her twenty-odd years older than Chambrun. A rumor that they had been lovers in the old days seemed unlikely. The staff was always trying to involve Chambrun in unlikely love affairs. Betsy Ruysdale was the only real possibility I was sure. Perhaps Victoria Haven reminded him of another time, another world that he remembered with pleasure, which would explain his relaxing of the rules in her case.

We walked through Chambrun's garden and across the roof to Penthouse Two. Victoria Haven opened the door almost before we knocked. I suspected she'd been looking out the window.

"Well, Pierre, it's about time," she said.

She is something to look at. Tall, straight as a ramrod, her hair, piled on top of her head, a gaudy red that God never invented. She wore a plain black dress, but she was decorated with enough rings and bracelets and necklaces to start a pawnshop.

"Don't tell me there's another bomb threat?" she said. Her voice was husky from a little too much liquor and a great many too many cigarettes. She was smoking one in a long holder now. "I will not go down to that goddamned gymnasium again. I'd rather be blown sky high!"

"No bomb threat, Victoria," Chambrun said. "May we come in? You know Mark Haskell."

She looked at me, her eyes as bright as the diamonds she was wearing. "I know him," she said. "How is that beautiful blond girl friend of yours, young man? I hate her, you know."

"Hate Shirley?"

"She's so damned beautiful," the old girl said. "At my age there's no way to compete. Well, don't just stand there. Come in."

I had never been in her penthouse before, and I had never seen anything like the room we entered. It looked like a glorified junk shop. There was twice as much furniture as the room could properly hold, most of it Victorian, as far as I could see. Heavy red velvet curtains blotted out the windows. Bookcases overflowed into stacks and piles of volumes on the floor. Sunday papers from the last six months were scattered about. Memories of the Collier brothers flashed into my mind, except that I saw at once there wasn't a speck of dust in the place. What appeared to be disorder was obviously order to Victoria Haven. I suspected if asked for it she could put her hand on the editorial page of the *Times* for last Christmas.

An asthmatic growl sounded from behind a whatnot loaded with Staffordshire dogs. A Japanese spaniel, luxuriating on a bright scarlet satin cushion, gave me an unfriendly leer.

"You have to get to know Toto before he will welcome you," Mrs. Haven said. "I was having my midday martini, Pierre. A little early perhaps, but I needed one after my experience in that gymnasium, with all those dumbbells. I'm not talking about people, but those ghastly exercise gadgets. Will you join me?"

Chambrun never drinks in the middle of the day, but, to my surprise, he said he would. I wasn't sorry. I could stand a drink about then.

She made martinis very expertly, and then, with a fresh cigarette in her holder, she settled comfortably in an over-stuffed armchair.

"Well, Pierre, it's about time somebody made something clear to me. Obviously they didn't expect to find a bomb here. They didn't look. I wouldn't have let them, by the way. It would have taken a month to overcome the disorder they'd have created."

He smiled at her, like an indulgent parent smiles at a precocious child. A strange relationship, but obviously a warm one.

"We were warned that there was a bomb in the wall safe in my apartment," he told her. "It turned out to be a harmless alarm clock, attached to nothing. We believe it was planted there night before last." He didn't say anything about masked men, or kidnappings, or country cottages.

"Some kind of practical joke?" the old woman asked.

"Possibly, but we'd like to find the joker," Chambrun said.

"So would I! A full hour in that gymnasium, I was. Poor Toto, he loathed it."

Poor Toto, at the mention of his name, made an angry gargling sound.

"We're not sure how the joker got into my penthouse," Chambrun said. "I came to see you because I hoped you might have seen someone on the roof who had no business there."

"No one," she said promptly. "Of course, there was Tim Gulliver. He looks after my garden in his off hours."

Tim Gulliver had been a maintenance man at the Beaumont for twenty years. A man to be trusted.

"I'm thinking more of after dark," Chambrun said.

Victoria Haven took a deep drag on her cigarette and promptly had a coughing fit. She used her martini, not the first, to cure it.

"I don't go peering around on the roof after dark with a flashlight," she said. "But night before last? There was one odd thing. At least I thought it was odd."

"Yes?" he said patiently.

"Lights in your penthouse at about nine fifteen. Stayed on for a good half hour."

"What's odd about that?" he asked.

"Oh Pierre, my dear Pierre! I've been living with your habits for a good thirty years. I know them as well as if—as if I were married to you!" She whooped with laughter. "You always dine in your office at nine o'clock. I don't think you've varied from that procedure five times since I've lived here. Excepting, of course, the winter of 1962 when you had pneumonia. So, night before last, I wondered idly what had changed your routine."

"That could be very helpful, Victoria," Chambrun said, "because I was having dinner in my office at nine o'clock. Could it have been the maids, do you think, turning down my bed?"

"The maids always get to you at ten o'clock," Mrs. Haven said. "They came that night, about fifteen minutes after those first lights went out. By the way, when are you going to invite me to dinner again? I've been dreaming of mussels in that special sauce the chef makes."

"You could order them for yourself, Victoria."

She gave him a flirtatious little smile. "That would not be the same as having them with you, old friend."

"Soon," he said.

We got up to go. The old woman had one last piece of information. "You asked about prowlers on the roof after dark, Pierre. I did not see anyone, but I can assure you there was no one."

"How do you know?"

"Toto cannot abide strangers. If he'd heard anything he would have raised holy hell!"

Toto seemed to confirm this by giving us an angry snarl as we walked past his satin cushion.

We hesitated outside Mrs. Haven's penthouse. It was a warm hazy day, a faint cloud of smog hanging over the city's towers.

"This was once a safe place to live," Chambrun said. "It has changed, Mark. There is violence at its core these days. Poverty turns people into animals."

I was more concerned with Mrs. Haven's information. "You think she was accurate?" I asked. "That would seem to place our man in your place shortly after nine."

"She is always accurate," he said. He smiled. "She has been keeping tabs on me for years."

We walked across the tar and gravel roof to the garden door of Penthouse Three. Jonathan Harkness, the Britisher, was there, enjoying a late breakfast or brunch served to him by room service. He was gracious, invited us in, offered us coffee, or a drink.

Chumbrun told him we'd just had martinis with Mrs. Haven.

"Which is my quota at lunchtime—perhaps for the next year," he said. "I have never been able to acquire the martinis-for-lunch habit. Perhaps a good thing for a man who has work to do."

Harkness was a tall, slender, well-muscled man, the classic picture of the British soldier-officer, down to the little tan toothbrush mustache. About fifty, I thought. The inevitable British pipe rested on the table beside him, ready to go.

"In my life," he said, "the martini at lunch is the prologue to a long nap. What can I do for you, Mr. Chambrun?"

"First, let me apologize for the inconvenience of this morning," Chambrun said.

"The bomb? I was happy to hear it was a false alarm."

"But it's my reason for being here," Chambrun said. He told Harkness the same story he'd given Mrs. Haven, leaving out his personal adventure. He added Mrs. Haven's observation about the lights in his penthouse shortly after nine. "Of course, if you weren't here that evening, Mr. Harkness, you won't be able to help me."

Harkness picked up his pipe and lit it. I thought there were faint lines of strain at the corner of his eyes.

"You do know that I was here," he said.

"How would I know?"

"I suppose room service told you that I had dinner served here that night."

"I didn't ask," Chambrun said.

"It will come out," Harkness said. "Very frankly, I have been waiting here for the police to appear."

Chambrun's eyebrows rose. "The police?"

"I had a lady here for dinner," Harkness said. "I suppose I should have reported it, but I needed time to think. Scandal is something I must avoid at this particular time in my life. You see, I am here on a diplomatic mission for Her Majesty's government."

"What is so scandalous about having a lady for dinner?"

"This particular lady," Harkness said. "It was Laura Kauffman."

Chambrun waited in silence.

"She was an old friend of my wife's and mine in England," Harkness said. His pipe wasn't going properly and he fiddled with his lighter for a moment. He was very obviously sparring for time. "I say 'friend,' but that implies more than I want it to," he went on. "She was part of the social swim in London for several seasons. Part of my job is to circulate at parties and balls and other events where people gather."

"Just what is your job, Mr. Harkness?" Chambrun asked. He sounded a shade less cordial than he'd been a moment ago. "From your registration card we have you down as 'industrialist,' what we call in this country 'big business.' "

Harkness turned his head, like a man looking for the nearest exit. "I think I must at least hint at the truth because I need your help, Mr. Chambrun. 'Big business' is what I believe is called a 'cover' for my real job. Oh, I am on the boards of several big corporations, carefully placed there by the people I really work for."

"Intelligence?" Chambrun asked.

Harkness nodded, biting down hard on the stem of

his pipe. One of the things that irritates Chambrun is to find that information on one of his registration cards is inaccurate. It indicates that Atterbury, Jerry Dodd, even Chambrun himself, has not done his job thoroughly.

"You spoke of help, Mr. Harkness," Chambrun said in a flat, cold voice.

"I would like not to be forced to expose what I have just told you to the police," Harkness said. "It could leak. That could undo months of difficult and very delicate work."

"But you have told us," Chambrun said.

"You have an enviable reputation for being a very decent and discreet man."

I could have told him that flattery would get him no place, but I let it ride.

"I have to have a reason for exercising discretion," Chambrun said.

Harkness got up and began to prowl the room, chewing on his pipe, hands jammed down in the pockets of his summer tweed jacket.

"Time is a luxury I don't have," Chambrun said.

Harkness faced him. He was, I thought, a strong man, not a frightened schoolboy trying to explain away some minor misdeed. I knew, somehow, that he wasn't a guilty husband about to tell us of some sexual game playing, even if the notorious Laura Kauffman had been his dinner companion.

"There are certain rules to the game I'm in," he said. "You don't let friendship, or women, or any other kind of personal indulgence take you off the main line. If a friend is drowning, you let him drown. To help him might be to reveal your real identity and make yourself useless. That is the rule I've broken."

Chambrun sat still and silent, his bright eyes buried in those deep pouches. He wasn't going to make it easy for Harkness.

"As you know," Harkness said, "Mrs. Kauffman had an international reputation as a hostess. She was always at the center of the gayest and biggest parties given wherever she happened to be. She knew everyone who is famous, and rich—in the public eye. She also had a reputation for being, shall I say, very free with her favors."

"That matches what I know of her," Chambrun said. He knew so much more that he wasn't revealing.

"My wife, Priscilla, and I came to know Laura Kauffman in London. We were both aware of the kind of high stakes game she was playing."

"Are you suggesting that she was an operator for some government?" Chambrun asked.

"No," Harkness said. "Her game was personal excitement. She collected men like a hunter collects and stuffs the heads of the beasts he kills. She was eager to have everyone know who her conquests had been. Women hated her because their men weren't safe if Laura got her hooks into them."

"You were one of them?" Chambrun asked.

Harkness gave us a short, sharp laugh. "Not even close," he said. "My wife happens to be the perfect partner for me. But there was someone whom I will simply refer to as my closest friend. School friend, college friend, and later in my department in the government. He was much younger than Laura, but that made him all the more desirable. He had no wife, no woman to whom he owed any loyalties. For him, Laura was a fascinating game to be played to the hilt. Somewhere along the way he fell in love with her, knowing all the while what she was. In that span of weakness—well, he talked too much."

"Secrets about his work?"

"I think—I hope—not secrets about anything specific, but certainly what his work is. That was all she needed."

"For what?"

"About a year went by and Laura had long since turned away from my friend to hunt in other areas. And then she sent for him. She had her eye on someone very high up in the government. This high-up is a very close friend of my friend. My friend must help her with this intrigue of hers or she would make public what she knew about him. My friend is caught in a bind. He must betray his friend or have his own career wrecked."

"This threat to your friend happened when?" Chambrun asked.

"Ten days ago," Harkness said. "Just before I was due to take off for New York."

"And you were supposed to do what?"

"Try to persuade Laura Kauffman to turn off the heat," Harkness said.

"You were in trouble, too, weren't you?" Chambrun asked. "If your friend talked about himself, and then sent you as an emmisary, weren't you in the same position as your friend? She had something on you, too?"

"Yes," Harkness said.

"So you invited her to dinner. Did she agree to 'turn off the heat'?"

Harkness's face was a hard, bitter mask. "She laughed at me," he said. "She suggested that I might have better luck pleading my case if I would join her in her suite later in the evening."

"And did you?" Chambrun asked, quietly.

"No, for God sake!" Harkness said.

"Not even to save a drowning friend and yourself?"

"No!"

Chambrun took one of his Egyptian cigarettes from the silver case he always carries and lit it. His eyes were narrowed against the smoke.

"You do need help, Mr. Harkness?" he asked.

Harkness produced a handkerchief and blotted at the little beads of sweat that had appeared on his forehead.

"I don't quite know why you have told me all this," Chambrun said. "Laura Kauffman is dead. Your friend is safe. You are safe."

"Because I cannot account for myself at the time she was murdered," Harkness said. "The homicide people will keep probing and probing until—" He spread his hands in a helpless gesture.

"We happen to know—" Chambrun hesitated. "We believe Laura Kauffman was alive at eleven o'clock, dead at twenty minutes to one." His hesitation and rewording must have meant he was wondering about Mayberry's story. Could she have been dead when Mayberry came out into the hall and found Chambrun there? According to the medical examiner it was possible. "But let's take it back a little, Mr. Harkness. Where were you, say, between ten o'clock and twenty minutes to one that night?"

"Laura came here to dine at eight o'clock," Harkness said. "She left about nine-thirty, laughing, and saying she hoped I might decide to join her later. The 'heat was off' until I made up my mind about that."

"And what did you do?"

"The innocent man's inevitable alibi that won't check," Harkness said. "This place smelled of her scent. I had to get away from it. I went out into the park and sat there for God knows how long—hours I think—trying to decide what to do."

"Whether or not to go to her suite and keep the ball in play?" Chambrun asked.

"I admit I thought of it," Harkness said. "It was a repulsive idea to me. But if an hour in bed with this woman would save my friend and me, couldn't I live with that? But I knew something. We were trapped forever, whatever I did. When she wanted something from either of us later on, we were hooked. I decided if the ship was to sink, it might as well be now as later. At least I could go back to my wife with a straight story."

"Did you think about killing her?" Chambrun asked, as casually as if he were asking about the weather.

Harkness looked straight at him. "Yes, I did," he said. "It's not as absurd as it sounds, Mr. Chambrun. Sex with her would simply have been a delaying action, get me nowhere in the long run. But if she were dead, my friend and I would be safe; the jobs we were involved in would be secure."

"You decided against it? Why?"

"I didn't think I could get away with it," he said.

"Why not? You had no problem getting to her in private. She'd invited you. All you had to do was get out after you'd killed her."

Harkness put down his cold pipe. "I have killed men in my time, Mr. Chambrun," he said. "In the army, once in my job. But somehow I couldn't imag-

ine killing a woman. Some sort of antiquated chivalry,
I suppose. I couldn't bring myself to think about it for
more than a moment."

"A question or two," Chambrun said. "Did you go
to the Cancer Fund Ball the next night?"

"Good God, no!" Harkness said.

"What you said about women hating Laura Kauffman," Chambrun said. "There must have been quite a
few gals there, perhaps members of her own committee, who are happier today than they were two days
ago."

"I don't think Laura gave a damn," Harkness said.

"Perhaps she should have. You've opened up a line
of thought for me, Harkness. The murder was so vio-
lent, so vicious that perhaps, as you suggested, some
sort of antiquated chivalry has kept us from thinking
of a woman as the killer. But a jealous woman—?" He
raised his shoulders in a Gallic shrug. "Any vestiges of
any beauty or sexual allure Laura Kauffman ever had
were eliminated, slashed and jabbed beyond recognition."

"She was a very ripe, fine-looking woman just a little time before that," Harkness said.

Chambrun rubbed out his cigarette in an ashtray.
"So, Mr. Harkness, Lieutenant Hardy will come here
to question you. He is a methodical man. Sooner or
later he will come across the fact that you entertained
Mrs. Kauffman here the night of the killing. Your
story will be that you invited her, an old friend from
London, to have dinner. She came about eight and
left about nine thirty. At a quarter to ten you went for
a walk in the park. You came back into the hotel
about two."

"Unhappily, there's no way to prove that," Harkness said.

"I think there will be," Chambrun said. "Someone will have seen you leave the hotel and noted the time. Someone will have seen you come back, and noted the time."

"That would be a miracle."

"No miracle," Chambrun said. "I will arrange it."

"Then you believe me?"

Chambrun stood up. He smiled at the Englishman. "I can always change my mind later," he said.

THREE

It was not like Chambrun to cross a friend, and Lieutenant Hardy was his friend. I felt uncomfortable at being in on a scheme to hide something from the homicide man. Chambrun evidently believed Harkness. I wasn't sure I did. But it was unlike him to throw up roadblocks to obstruct a friend.

I should have known better.

Hardy was in Chambrun's office when we returned there. He explained he was waiting for one of his men to bring James Kauffman down from the infirmary. Dr. Partridge had said he thought Kauffman could stand up under questioning this afternoon. It was afternoon, going on toward three o'clock.

Chambrun sat down and gestured toward the Turkish coffee maker. I went over to it and poured his usual demitasse. He was looking very pleased with himself, I thought.

"I've just finished planning to manufacture some false evidence for you, Walter," he said.

Hardy just grinned at him.

"I've been talking with Jonathan Harkness who is occupying Penthouse Three on the roof, guest of the management," Chambrun said.

"He's next on my list," Hardy said. "Did you know

he entertained Laura Kauffman for dinner in his rooms the night of the murder?"

"I know that and a lot more," Chambrun said. He then proceeded to tell Hardy the entire story. I should have known he would. When he came to the end he said: "I find I believe his story, at least for now. If you try to dig it out of him, it will go in your report to headquarters. The nature of his job should be protected, I think, until we have reason to assume he's guilty. I suggest you accept his surface story. He dined the lady, she left, he spent a couple of hours on a warm summer evening in the park."

"I don't know," Hardy said, frowning.

"I will arrange for Mike Maggio, our night bell captain, to have seen him go out and come in at the times he says he did. That will cover you in your report on Harkness."

"Faking an alibi?"

"Everyone in this hotel knows what I'm doing every hour of the day and night," Chambrun said. "Nobody else has that kind of coverage. Harkness needs protection at the moment. I'd like to give it to him. He may be helpful to us before we're through."

"You know what would happen to you if the top brass finds out you've faked an alibi for him?" Hardy asked.

"A couple of years in the slammer," Chambrun said cheerfully.

"I'll go along," Hardy said after a moment.

Chambrun looked at me, his eyes dancing. "Feel better, Mark?"

He'd been aware of exactly what I'd been thinking. I should have known that, too.

Hardy brought his fist down on the arm of the

chair he was lounging in. "I would never have made a good juggler," he said. "Keeping two balls in the air at the same time doesn't suit my style. Or my talents. Laura Kauffman is my job, but I find my mind wandering over to you, Pierre. Have you got even a smell of the reasons for what happened to you?"

"Only the obvious," Chambrun said. "Someone wanted me away from the hotel so that something could happen without my seeing or knowing about it. So far the only out-of-the-way thing that's happened is your murder, and I was in the hotel when it happened! Whatever I wasn't supposed to see is no longer here for me to see, so I was set free."

"In this hotel the only thing that comes and goes, that changes, is people," I said.

Chambrun gave me a long, steady look. "I think that's bingo, Mark," he said. He pressed a button on his desk and Ruysdale came in from her office. "Tell Atterbury I want a list of everyone who has checked in since I was carted off, and everyone on that list who checked out before I got back."

Ruysdale went off without a word.

"How many would that be?" Hardy asked.

"Not so very many," Chambrun said. "We're full up, booked well in advance. People don't often come here for overnight, Walter. Too expensive. They book in advance, they stay for several days, a week, more. A one-night stand, which this must have been, shouldn't be hard to spot."

Hardy shook his head. "But a thousand people come and go every day who aren't registered," he said. "People who use the bars, the restaurants, the shops, attend the special functions. How many people were at that Cancer Fund Ball? Seven hundred? Eight hundred? If someone wanted to circulate in the hotel without your knowing it, he wouldn't, for God sake, register. It was important enough to him to have you out of the way to risk having to kill you, to risk a kidnapping charge, to have himself—or his hired professional—caught burglarizing your penthouse. If your seeing him was that dangerous to him, he surely wouldn't sign his name for you to see later."

"A 'John Smith,' " I said. It's a slang phrase we use in the business for someone who registers under a false name. It's not always in any way sinister. A movie star who wants privacy and no involvement with the press, a foreign diplomat who wants anonymity. There is another variety, of course, which every hotel knows about—the man who registers with a chick he shouldn't be with signs "Mr. and Mrs. John Smith" or some other phony. A suspicious wife has no evidence that way. We screen that kind pretty well, but now and then one of them gets by us.

"Maybe," Chambrun said. He lit one of his flat cigarettes. "If we're close, this person had to be here for some unhealthy reason. If I saw him—or her—I must know something that I could use against him. That's why I had to be removed. That suggests a 'John Smith' or no registration at all. Where would I have certainly been the day or night after I was kidnapped? At the Cancer Fund Ball." His smile was bitter. "Making sure my instructions were carried out and that everything went smoothly. It seems to me to be a very good bet that my enemy was attending the ball."

"And it's very likely that Laura Kauffman's murderer was there too," Hardy said. "He—or she, as you put it—was someone close to Laura, someone she let

into her rooms. Someone whose absence at the ball
might be noticed. Could be, you know."

"A very long shot," Chambrun said. "Remember,
the person who killed Laura was here in the hotel
while I was still in circulation. I could have seen him.
I was actually on the twenty-first floor close to the
time of the murder. It was hours later that I was removed. I have to believe the murderer didn't think my
seeing him somewhere in the hotel was a danger.
Someone else, someone who was to come on the scene
later, did."

"We've got the haystack," Hardy said, "but we don't
know what we're looking for in it."

I went down the hall to my apartment. I hadn't had
a shave, or a shower, or a change of clothes since the
night before. I expected, or rather hoped, to find Shirley there. She wasn't. This time she hadn't left me a
note. Well, she had a column to do. I called her at her
apartment and got no answer. She was probably
somewhere you go to look for gossip.

I was a little like Hardy when it came to trying to
keep two balls in the air at the same time. I kept
trying, in my mind, to link the kidnapping to the murder. It would be a hell of a lot simpler if we were only
looking for one person. But things like this aren't
usually arranged to be simple.

I couldn't let go of one suggestion that had been
made. The man who'd kidnapped Chambrun was a
professional, a man who knew locks and combina-
tions, a man prepared to kill if he had to. Was this
masked and gloved man the person Chambrun might
recognize? Somehow I didn't think so. That left us
with the professional's employer, the real villain of the

piece. When this setup was first suggested I had jumped eagerly at Mayberry as the most likely. He was a loud-mouthed phony who would go to extremes to get what he wanted. But there was no reason for him to have Chambrun removed except the silly business of the camera on the dance floor. Was he stupid enough to risk murder and a kidnapping charge just for that? And certainly Chambrun didn't have to be kept out of sight so he wouldn't see Mayberry. He knew Mayberry all too well, and his presence in the hotel was an unfortunate daily happening. After Mayberry I came up against a blank wall.

Looking and feeling more human, I went down the hall to my office. My secretary wasn't there and I realized it was quitting time for her.

Well, I was still being the big detective. The vice-chairman of the ball committee was a Mrs. Birdwell. I had her home phone number and I called her. She was eager to know if anything had developed in the Kauffman case. I told her there was nothing.

"But that's why I called you, Mrs. Birdwell," I said. "Is there a list of the guests who actually attended the ball?"

She said there was. "You had to have a ticket to get in," she said. "The tickets were checked off at the door against the list of contributors. There are eight hundred and forty names on it. It's at the Cancer Fund headquarters."

"What about gate crashers?" I asked her. "I mean, after people checked in they came and went, maybe to one of the bars outside the ballroom, to the ladies' or mens' rooms."

"You got a passout check if you left the ballroom," she said. "You couldn't get back in without it."

"What about buying tickets at the door?"

"There may have been a few, but they would be on the list."

"So there was no one there who wouldn't be on the list?" I asked.

"Oh, yes, there were others," Mrs. Birdwell said. "The press, for example. The radio and television people. They had their own passes, I suppose. Perhaps someone has a record of them, I don't know. They were, supposedly, kept in the press gallery. Then there were the movie people. They aren't on the guest list, of course. Except Mr. Herman and Mr. Duval, both of whom made handsome contributions to the fund."

So that was that. There was an airtight list, except it leaked at every pore. I wasn't doing so well as a detective. Well, Chambrun and Hardy weren't exactly balls of fire at this moment, I told myself. They'd dug up some facts about a very gaudy lady who'd gotten herself slaughtered. From what Harkness had told us we knew she was up to blackmail for her own exotic reasons. She'd tried it once too often, one had to believe.

At that moment I was so close to a central truth that it makes me sick to think of it now. If I hadn't been trying to be a smart aleck and had thought it through I might have prevented a tragedy that has left a mark on me for the rest of time.

I had a job, and, for all the balls in the air, I had to do it. That was the name of the game, working for Chambrun. Along about five o'clock, which it now was, people begin to swarm into the Beaumont's bars for that drink or two between work and home. The Trapeze Bar is probably the most popular gathering place for this hour. It is at the mezzanine level, just above the lobby. Some artist of the Calder school had decorated it with mobiles of circus performers. The exquisitely made little wire figures of trapeze acrobats moved gently in the air stirred up by the air-conditioning system. It's a smart room for smart people. The women are usually eye-catching, what society reporters have come to call "the beautiful people." The men are well tailored, from conversative Brooks Brothers to the very mod designers. They all smell of money. They all have money or they wouldn't be in the Beaumont.

At about five I begin to circulate through the active rooms, aiming to hit the Trapeze last. I am supposed to be looking for familiar faces, customers who have been turning up for years at these way stations. I have learned which ones wish to be greeted, which ones wish to be ignored. Often there are famous people, movie stars, stage stars, United Nations luminaries, local political figures. I must decide whether to pass the word along to the gossip professionals, like Shirley. "Seen at the Trapeze Bar in the Beaumont last night was the glamorous Miss Whooziz being squired by Mr. McSchmoe, the well-known continental playboy." A lot of people go to places like the Trapeze just to be seen, and they feel cheated if nobody notices. Others—and I have to make the judgment—would consider a gossip column item an invasion of privacy.

Most of the people in the Trapeze that late afternoon I'd seen there hundreds of times before. I was about to slide up to the bar for a drink when I noticed a man sitting alone at a corner table. It was Chester Cole, the public relations man for Duval's film. He was hiding behind the dark glasses he seemed to wear night and day.

"I thought all you people had taken off for the coast," I said, as I reached his table.

"Buy you a drink?" he asked.

"Only the call girls around here get drinks bought for them by the customers," I said. "Let you in on a secret. I don't have to pay for drinks in this place."

"Well, sit down anyway," he said.

I sat with my back to the wall where I could watch the comings and goings. I nodded to an approaching waiter. They all knew my five o'clock drink was a Jack Daniel's on the rocks with a splash of water.

"Only the glittering ones went to the coast," Cole said. "Clark Herman has a finished picture that's opening here in a couple of days. I stayed behind to give it a push." The black glasses turned my way. "You're the one with stories to tell."

"Let's see, how does it go?" I said. "'The police expect an early arrest.'"

"A real crazy doll from all accounts, your Mrs. Kauffman," he said. "Hollywood is shaking in its boots."

"Oh?"

"A hatful of big-name male stars have, it is said, been involved with the lady in the past." Cole laughed. "They're all rushing around trying to set up alibis for themselves. The ones making films out of the country are thanking their lucky stars. I'd have to guess the police are suffering from too many possible suspects, not too few."

"Right about now Homicide is talking to the husband," I said. "He's probably adding to the list. What about your stable? Anybody there worried?"

Cole gave me a sardonic smile. "You can write off our glamorous leading man. He isn't the type."

"We have Robert Randle pegged," I said, remembering the registration card with the letter G written on it. "Let me tell you, the police aren't writing off women. Women hated her, women whose men go involved with our Laura."

"You can forget about Janet Parker," Cole said. "She's the old-fashioned type. She's been quietly married to her high school boy friend for the last ten years. A lot of us have tried and been laughed off, including your friend Mayberry. What a clown!"

"What about the big shots, Herman and Duval?" I asked.

"I got the impression that neither of them had ever met her until they arrived here at the hotel," Cole said. "I know they both talked to her, trying to get her help in changing Chambrun's mind about the filming at the ball."

"I don't imagine our Laura wasted any time with new men if they appealed to her," I said.

"I don't know about Clark Herman," Cole said, "but I was present when Duval talked to her." He laughed. "He didn't go to see her, you understand. Had her brought to him. He was at his disagreeable best. He didn't ask, he made demands. A genius makes demands. He was about as unpleasant as a big shot as you can imagine. He was waving a fifty-thousand-dollar donation to the fund under her nose, and it was going to be his way or else. I would guess he was about as attractive to her as a hooded cobra. In any case, he's about as old as she was, or a year or two older. I understand her present taste was for younger ones."

I grinned at him. "What about you? You belong in that younger group."

He made a wry face. "I like to make my own passes," he said.

The waiter brought my drink—and a message. Chambrun wanted to see me in his office. I excused myself, and, carrying my drink, I went out a rear door of the Trapeze to the second floor corridor.

Ruysdale wasn't in her office, and I went straight through into Chambrun's sanctum. He was sitting at his desk, and Ruysdale was over by the windows looking at the park. There was something curiously tense about the atmosphere. I had seen that look of dark anger on Chambrun's face before. I wondered what I had done wrong.

"You sent for me, boss?" I asked.

His heavy lids lifted and he looked at me. I could have sworn there was something like pain in that look.

"I have some bad news for you, Mark," he said.

I was fired, I thought. "It would be nice to know what I've done," I said.

"You haven't done anything, Mark," he said. "It's your Miss Thomas."

"Shirley?"

"She's dead," Chambrun said.

I couldn't take it in. I didn't believe it.

"I'm sorry," Chambrun said. "I wish to God that was more than just a word."

The room started to spin around me. I remember I dropped my drink on his Persian rug. Ruysdale was coming toward me from the window, her hands held out in friendship and compassion.

PART 3

ONE

Someone young, and vital, and close to you simply cannot die. It had to be some grotesque joke, and yet I knew that, coming from Chambrun, it couldn't be.

Ruysdale, her hands cool and reassuring, guided me to one of the leather armchairs. I didn't resist sitting down because my legs were about not to hold me up. A moment later she handed me a shot glass full of liquor. I drank it, and it burned like fire. All the while Chambrun sat hunched in his desk chair, his bright black eyes watching me with a rare sympathy.

I guess he decided I was ready for it and he gave it to me. There had been a call from Bernice Braden, a girl who did secretarial work for Shirley. She was obviously hysterical and she had called Chambrun because she didn't know what to do, and Shirley had told her on the phone that morning that if there were any sort of emergency she should call. Bernice is a nice girl, married, with a couple of kids, who types and machine-copies Shirley's column for syndication. It helps add to the Braden family's income. She comes and goes, collecting copy from Shirley, letting herself in and out with her own key to the apartment. That was why Shirley and I had used my apartment for our

thing together. Bernice was apt to show up at odd
times. She had no regular schedule.

I tried to concentrate on what Chambrun was telling me.

Bernice had let herself into the apartment about a
quarter past four, a little more than an hour ago. The
place was a shambles. Shirley was there, dead. She
had some kind of awful wound in her head.

"According to Mrs. Braden, every scrap of paper in
the place had been burned in the open fireplace,"
Chambrun said. "Correspondence, files on people and
events Shirley kept in metal cabinets. Her job to collect anything and everything on people with any news
value."

I struggled up out of the chair. I had to go to her.

"No point, Mark," Chambrun said. "They will have
taken her to the medical examiner's office by now."

My legs gave out and I slumped down into the chair
again. My eyes stung, and I realized that tears were
running down my cheeks.

"Hardy was here when we got the word," Chambrun said. He was feeding me little bits and pieces, I
suppose to keep me from concentrating on the central
horror. "It's not his case but he feels responsible in a
way."

"Responsible?"

"He had asked Shirley to dig up everything she
could find on Laura Kauffman, in her files, from her
sources. It was his notion that someone would appear
on a list she could compile who could be placed here
in the hotel on the night Mrs. Kauffman was killed."

"Oh, God!" I said.

"Hardy's at Shirley's apartment now," Ruysdale
said. She had brought me another drink. "We should

hear from him soon. Dear Mark, I wish there was something sensible for me to do or say."

It came pouring out of me then. I was choking on the words. She wasn't just a little tramp I'd shacked up with for the sexual delights she'd offered. She was gay, open, undevious, a marvelous companion.

"She wasn't like the other garbage collectors who do gossip columns," I heard myself saying. "She never wrote things that would hurt people. She left the rotten stuff to others. Why, for Christ sake? She was so in love with life—and living!"

"Not a nice world we live in," Chambrun said.

"What the hell do you care?" I shouted at him. "It didn't happen in your lousy hotel!"

Ruysdale's cool hand rested against my cheek. "Easy, Mark," she said.

Of course I was off my rocker. Chambrun cared. He cared because he was my friend, because he hated violence. I had to yell at someone. I had to *do* something! I realized that the hot, burning feeling in my gut was not the result of a second straight slug of whiskey. It was a rage so intense I might die of it if I didn't do something. Somewhere there was some sonofabitch who had done this awful thing to a nice, decent girl and I was going to find him and kill him.

"I've got to go over there," I said. "I've got to dig out every single fact there is, and then I'm going to—"

"Mark!" Chambrun's voice was sharp. It stopped me after I'd taken two steps toward the door. "I know how you feel," he said, gently now. "Let me tell you, you have to be detached to make any sense in a situation like this. Leave it to the people who aren't personally hurt by it—Hardy, whoever is in charge of the case. Let them put the pieces together. They will, you know. All you can do in your state of mind is muddy the waters."

"I have to go to her," I said. "Wherever she is, she's all alone."

"She's dead, Mark."

It wouldn't have hurt any more if he'd hit me over the head with a sledge hammer. I swayed back to the chair and crumpled down in it again. I couldn't get things separated in my aching skull. I could see her, and smell her, and feel her warm skin against mine, and her tender arms around me. I could see the love in her eyes and feel her happy, passionate response to my lovemaking. I could see us walking arm in arm down Fifth Avenue on a spring day, window shopping like children outside a candy store. I could hear her laughing at our private jokes. I remembered how men looked at her and how they envied me.

There had been bits and scraps about our pasts as we lay together in the night. Where was it she had grown up? Somewhere in New England, wasn't it? I seemed to recall that her father had died of a heart attack while she was in college. Her mother? I couldn't remember anything about her, or the mention of any sisters or brothers. Someone would have to be notified. Bernice Braden might know.

"Family," I said, still choking on tears.

"Mrs. Braden doesn't know of any," Ruysdale said.

"Maybe she had a will," I said. "Someone has to make arrangements for—for—"

"All in good time," Chambrun said.

"Of all the people I know in the world she deserved this less than anyone," I said.

"No one deserves violence," Chambrun said, his

voice gone cold. "Even a blackmailing bitch like Laura Kauffman didn't deserve what she got."

How could he think of anyone else but Shirley? How could he mention Laura Kauffman in the same context? What else was there to think about but Shirley and the bastard who'd killed her?

The little red light blinked on the phone at Chambrun's elbow. He let Ruysdale take it.

"Hardy," she said.

Chambrun leaned forward and switched on the squawk box. "I've got you on the box, Walter," he said. "Mark's here with us."

"Jesus, Mark, I'm sorry," Hardy said.

I blubbered something unintelligible.

"Sergeant Caldwell is in charge here," Hardy said. "Good man. One of the best. So far there isn't much. It was a gunshot; damn near blew the top of her head off."

I heard a kind of quavering cry. It came from me.

"Everything Miss Thomas ever committed to paper has been destroyed, burned in the fireplace," Hardy said. "He took his time after the shooting. Desk, files, everything ransacked. Books taken off the shelves as if he might be looking for something hidden in them. You have to guess he didn't find what he was looking for, but he made sure he hadn't overlooked it and left it behind. Mark, do you know anything about family?"

I shook my head.

"He doesn't know," Chambrun said.

"Did she have a lawyer? Was she religious? Did she have a priest, a minister, who might know about family? The secretary doesn't know."

"We didn't talk about lawyers or God," I heard myself say.

"The syndicate that handled her column might have answers," Chambrun said. "Mrs. Braden should be able to put you on to them."

"Good idea," Hardy said. He hesitated. "There's one sort of far-out coincidence, Pierre. The gun that killed her was a .44 caliber handgun."

I didn't get it for a moment. Then I remembered it was a .44 that Chambrun's abductor had carried.

"No way to connect the two guns," Hardy said. "As far as we know your man didn't fire his gun anywhere, so there's nothing for ballistics. But it's an oddity."

"In order to protect the rights of the great American sportsman we don't have any decent gun laws," Chambrun said. "There are probably thousands of those .44's available to any creep who wants one."

"I know," Hardy said. "But the coincidence is worth bearing in mind, Pierre. Be seeing you."

Shirley, it turned out, had made a new will a couple of months ago. She'd used her syndicate's lawyer to draw it up for her. She had left everything she had to me, for God sake. There wasn't any money to speak of. She'd been too young to be concerned about old age. But all her books, her papers—which were now nonexistent—the stuff in her apartment, were left to me. She'd never mentioned it to me. Why should she? She hadn't dreamed of dying. She was immortal, just as all of us are when we think of ourselves.

She had left me one obligation. I was to see to it that she was cremated.

I can't really put times together. I know it was evening when I got to the city morgue with an authority from the lawyer. They're pretty cold-blooded in the morgue, but the guy who handled me had some feelings. The keep the bodies in sort of icebox drawers. We stopped by the one that had Shirley's name on it.

"If you cared about her, you won't want to look at her," the man said. "Official identification was made by her secretary."

Poor Bernice Braden. I realized I didn't want to see anything that would blur my memory of what she'd been. I turned away from the box. I still had my Shirley, alive and laughing and loving. I made arrangements for the cremation, and that was that.

A light summer rain was falling when I walked out onto the street. Where to go? What to do? Who to talk to? There was only the Beaumont, and Chambrun and Ruysdale. I walked what seemed miles in the rain. I must have been a sight when I walked through the revolving door from the street into the Beaumont's lobby, my hair matted, my suit waterlogged.

Mike Maggio, the night bell captain, had me by the arm and was steering me to the elevator. He is a mischievous, smiling Italian who, for the first time I could remember, looked dead serious. He went upstairs with me, took my key from my shaking hands, and opened the door to my apartment. I was to take a steaming hot shower while he made me a drink. I got out of my clothers and into the shower. When I came out and had toweled myself down, I went to my closet for a bathrobe. There, hanging right in front, was a negligee Shirley kept there. I sat down on the floor, stark naked, and cried. Mike Maggio let me weep it out.

Then, after I'd had the drink Mike made me, believe it or not, I slept on the couch in my living room.

I couldn't face the bed where she had been only the night before.

If you've ever been through that kind of experience, and I hope to God you haven't, you'll know that nothing is stable. You tell yourself you have to go about your regular routines, and you do, in a mechanical fashion, but every now and then your grief sweeps over you in waves, literally doubling you up with pain. I woke up, bones aching, a little after midnight. For about ten seconds I wondered why I was there on the couch, and then it came over me like a nausea. I wanted to get out of the apartment. She was everywhere.

Normally there were things to do at this time of night. It wasn't much better out in the real world. I should have known that Shirley's death had already been on radio and TV. Everyone who knew me and of my connection with her had words of sympathy. And questions! Did I have any idea who might have done it? Did I know why it was done? Reporters, still hanging around for some news in the Kauffman case, had something new to occupy them. Me. They followed me around like the tail of a kite as I went from the Blue Lagoon, to the Spartan, to the Trapeze.

In the Trapeze I was astonished to see Chester Cole, the PR man for Duval's film, still sitting where I'd left him at that corner table, hours and hours ago. He looked stiff drunk to me, or maybe it was just that he hadn't moved for so long. Five o'clock I'd left him, one o'clock now. I asked Eddie, the head bartender, about him.

"I don't know where he puts it," Eddie said. "Must have drunk two quarts of Irish whiskey. Doesn't show it, though. Just signals for another double."

I walked over to the table. "The bartender says you have a hollow leg," I said.

The black glasses looked up at me. "I'm sorry about your girl," he said. His speech wasn't thick, just a little overprecise. But he hit me where I was living at that moment.

"I'd just as soon not talk about it," I said.

"Understandable," he said. "You ever do jigsaw puzzles?"

"When I was four, with my grandmother," I said.

"I've been doing one for hours," he said. "Ever since you left me."

It didn't make sense. "Mine was Napoleon at Waterloo," I said.

He laughed, as though what I'd said was much funnier than I thought it was. "I guess you could call mine that, too," he said.

So two quarts of Irish had done its work, I thought.

"I've got no place to go," he said. "I lose this job I've got with Herman Productions and the only place to go is down. What do I care about Laura Kauffman, a crazy, sex-mad doll? But I saw you dancing with your girl at the ball. She was something else again."

"I just can't talk about her now, Chester," I said. I was being buried under one of those waves of self-pity.

"You seen anyone around lately who reminds you of Napoleon?" he asked.

The Irish whiskey talking again, I thought.

His smile was twisted. "I might just decide to bring about his Waterloo—on account of your girl."

"Who the hell are you talking about?" I asked.

"Napoleon," he said. "Who else got the works at Waterloo?" He drew a deep breath. "Couple of pieces

still don't fit. But don't get lost, Mark. I may be able
to show you the finished product any time now. Your
girl deserves it."

He was getting to me. "If you know something—"

"I need time to figure out why I feel like being a
hero," he said. "But I'll leave you with a question.
Who do I know anything about in this cockeyed world
of yours?"

"The film people," I said, "who are no longer here."

"That's the joker," he said. "Are they or are they
not?"

He stood up, gave me a stiff, formal little bow and
walked, straight as a ramrod, out of the Trapeze.

I have a lot of pretty good friends who come and go
at the Beaumont, but that night, of all nights, none of
them seemed to come in. Perhaps it was for the best.
It would have meant telling the same unfinished story
over and over.

I went up to Chambrun's office and found it
locked. I checked with Miss Kiley and learned that
the "No more calls except in an emergency" rule was
in play. The boss had turned in. He hadn't had any
real sleep for a long time. I couldn't by any stretch of
the imagination classify Chester Cole's crazy talk as
an emergency.

I felt so goddamned lonely! For months now, when
the day's work was over, there had been Shirley to
gripe to, to laugh with, to love. No more. Not ever.

Ruysdale? She could be up in Chambrun's penthouse with him. I never had known where her private
hideout was. There was an emergency unlisted number for her, but no address to go with it. She would
have listened with patience and understanding while I

went round and round about Shirley. But I wasn't, or shouldn't let myself be, an emergency.

I tried to get Lieutenant Hardy on his home phone but he didn't answer. It would be legitimate for me to call to ask if there was anything new. He wasn't at Police Headquarters. The best I could do there was leave a message I'd called. He'd know why.

In the end I went to my apartment. I had to face it sometime. In the morning I would pack up Shirley's things and deep-six them somewhere. Having them around would make the pain a little too exquisite.

I slept on the couch again.

I woke up about eight o'clock, my usual time. You get so you have a kind of internal alarm clock. It was another day, a hotel to run—a man to find and punish. The impulse to tears was gone, the burning rage. In their place was a kind of cold determination. Everything else in my life, from now on, came second to finding the man who had shot Shirley. Nothing else mattered a damn.

I made coffee and toast in my kitchenette. I didn't have an appetite for more. At a few minutes after nine, shaved and dressed for this new day, I went down the hall to the main place. Ruysdale was at her desk as I had found her on hundreds of other mornings. She gave me a look and decided that the time for sweet talk and sympathy was past. She was right.

The boss was having breakfast of course. Didn't he always? Ruysdale thought I should go in. Hardy was there.

Chambrun was working on one of his breakfast favorites, a salmon steak with Bernaise sauce.

"Glad you came in, Mark," he said. "Hardy has a question for you."

Hardy looked his usual self. The sonsofbitches had all had their normal quota of sleep without nightmares. Hardy was sitting at the table with Chambrun, toying with a cup of coffee. Across the room M. Fresney, the chef, stood expressionless, behind the serving table. He looked disappointed, really, as if Chambrun had passed up some special work of art he'd provided for this morning. He pointed to the coffee service and I nodded that I would.

"The Shirley Thomas case isn't mine," Hardy said. He sounded as though he was talking about some distant case in China somewhere. A distant place, a nonperson. Perhaps they'd decided that was the way to handle it with me. The Shirley Thomas case!

"So it isn't your case," I said.

"But there may be a connection with what is my case," Hardy said. "You see, I'd asked her to dig up what she could on Laura Kauffman. The husband has given us so many names that it's worse than none. No place to start. Now, I have no way of knowing what Miss Thomas had in her files, nor who she may have talked to here in the city, in person or on the phone. But the telephone company has provided us with two numbers she called yesterday afternoon, not long after she went home to hunt for me. The first was an overseas call to a Miss Grace Peyron in Paris."

"She's a correspondent for *The Paris Herald*," I said. "An old friend. She ran down stories for Shirley abroad."

"I know," Hardy said. "We've talked to her. Miss Thomas asked her to dig out anything she could about Laura Hemmerly, Laura von Holtzmann, Laura Kauffman, going all the way back to the war. That was in line with what I'd asked for."

"The second call is more interesting," Chambrun said.

"The second call was to Hollywood, to Claude Duval," Hardy said. "The call was put through, because her phone was charged for it. I just finished talking to Duval. He didn't get her call personally. He has one of those automatic answering services attached to his phone. 'When you hear the buzzer leave your name, your phone number, your message.' He came home well after midnight, he says, which would have been four, five o'clock our time this morning. Shirley Thomas had called, left her number, and asked him to call collect. He had been planning to do so this morning at a decent hour. He had no idea why she'd called. He was shocked to hear what had happened to her."

"Do you have any idea why she called him, Mark?" Chambrun asked.

I shook my head. Something was bothering me.

"We called back Miss Peyron in Paris," Hardy said. "I thought perhaps she'd suggested Duval as some sort of source for Miss Thomas. She hadn't. Miss Thomas hadn't mentioned Duval to her."

It clicked. "Napoleon," I said.

"Napoleon?"

I had an absrud impulse to giggle. "Something funny happened on the way to the forum," I said.

"Cut it out, Mark," Chambrun said.

I told them about my strange conversation with Chester Cole last night. The talk about his jigsaw puzzle which could also be called 'Napoleon at Waterloo'; about his impulses to be a hero on Shirley's behalf; about how maybe all the film people hadn't gone. " 'That's the joker,' he said. 'Are they or are they not?' "

Chambrun's look froze me. "You didn't think this was worth reporting until now?" he asked.

"He was drunk! Two quarts of Irish whiskey, Eddie told me. I don't know how he managed to walk out of the place. It all sounded like drunken idiocy."

Chambrun pushed back his chair and stood up. "I think we'd better have a talk with Mr. Cole," he said.

The front desk gave us his room number on the ninth floor, and we went in search of Chester Cole. Ringing his doorbell and knocking on the door didn't produce any results. Chambrun went down the hall to the maids' pantry and came back with a passkey. We opened the door and found Cole standing just inside it. He could have been waiting there, hoping the trouble, whatever it was, would evaporate. He looked the way he ought to look, I told myself; red-eyed, disheveled. He was a man with a ghastly hangover. He had a seersucker robe pulled around his bony frame.

"What the hell is this? Some kind of raid?" he asked.

"We have to talk to you, Mr. Cole," Chambrun said, briskly. "This is Lieutenant Hardy of Homicide. You know Mark."

"Do you let yourself in anywhere you choose?" Cole asked. "If I don't answer my doorbell, it's because I don't want to answer it."

"A man who thinks about being a hero could be in trouble," Chambrun said. "I was concerned for your safety, Mr. Cole."

Cole backed into his room. From the bureau he picked up his black glasses. He seemed to feel more secure once he was hidden behind them. "I don't understand any of this," he said. "Hero?"

"You had a conversation with Mark last night," Chambrun said.

"Ah yes, in the Trapeze, wasn't it, late in the after-noon?"

"And again much later at night," I said, "after you'd taken on a couple of quarts of Irish."

His thin mouth moved in a forced smile. "I'm afraid I did rather tie one on," he said. "I'm afraid I don't remember our second visit together—if we had one, Mark."

"We talked about jigsaw puzzles and Napoleon at Waterloo," I said.

"It doesn't sound very elevating," he said. "I'm sorry, Mark, but I just don't remember."

"Very convenient for you, Mr. Cole," Chambrun said. "You don't remember considering being a hero."

"Hero about what?" he asked.

"You were going to help me—about Shirley," I said.

"Shirley?"

"Shirley Thomas, my girl!" I said. I was suddenly steaming.

A nerve twitched at the corner of his mouth. "I remember hearing," he said. "I'm terribly sorry about it, Mark."

"You told me you might have answers," I said. "You told me not to get lost, that you might be able to put it all together. You said Shirley deserved your help! Come on, Chester. You can't have forgotten all that!"

"My God, I must have been really stewed," he said. "Put what together? How could I help?"

"Put together your jigsaw puzzle. You said you'd been working on it for hours. 'Napoleon at Waterloo.' You asked me who you knew here at the Beaumont. The film people, you said. I said they were all gone except you. And you said, 'That's the joker. Are they or are they not?' "

"So what movie people are not gone?" Chambrun asked.

Cole gave a helpless little shrug. "Duval and Herman both went straight to Hollywood. Janet Parker and Bob Randle were supposed to head west sometime yesterday afternoon."

"The crew, the camera people?" Chambrun asked.

"They're all still on the film, all headed west," Cole said.

"So what the hell were you talking about?" I demanded.

"Just being a drunken bigshot, I guess," he said.

"You asked me if I'd seen anyone around who reminded me of Napoleon," I said. "You said you were thinking of bringing about his Waterloo. Who were you talking about, Chester?"

He gave me a helpless look.

"Duval?" Chambrun asked. "I gather he's a sort of Napoleonic figure in the film world."

"We talked about him earlier in the Trapeze," I said. "You weren't drunk then, Chester. You remember that?"

He nodded. "I told you about his summoning Mrs. Kauffman to his suite and behaving like a bastard," he said. "That's par for the course for him. He is a bastard."

"He knew Mrs. Kauffman?" Hardy asked, joining in for the first time.

"Not before that meeting, I think," Cole said. "She was chairman of the ball committee. He wanted her to get some of your rules changed, Mr. Chambrun. He didn't 'want,' he demanded."

"How old is Duval?" Hardy asked.

"Early sixties," Cole said. "That's just a guess."

"I'm trying to figure out why Miss Thomas called him long distance," Hardy said. "I'd asked her to go back on Mrs. Kauffman as far as she could—back to the war. A Frenchman Duval's age could have known her then, when she was Laura Hemmerly. Miss Thomas was on a fishing expedition. It may have cost her her life."

"You have a photograph of Duval?" Chambrun asked Cole.

"There are no photographs of him," Cole said.

"A Hollywood bigshot without photographs?"

"It's a fetish with him," Cole said. "No photographs. Everyone connected with him knows that. There have been incidents. He's smashed news cameras when photographers tried to get a shot of him."

"He looks like Telly Savalas the actor," I said.

That didn't seem to ring any bells with Chambrun.

"Who are you afraid of, Mr. Cole?" he asked.

"Afraid?"

"Sober, you've decided not to help. That suggests you're afraid of someone, of what might happen if you did."

"I tell you, I was just being a drunken bigshot," Cole said. "If I said all those things Mark says I said, I was being a phony. Maybe it pleased me to pretend I could do something to help Mark."

"Maybe you're the one who needs help, Mr. Cole," Chambrun said. "If you do, there's a way to get it from us."

"How?" Cole asked.

"By telling us the truth," Chambrun said.

TWO

Time wasn't any longer a factor with me. It wasn't as though Shirley was in danger and I had to do something before it was too late. It was already too late. Unfortunately, I had time to find the facts, to build a case, with or without help. And when I found my man! Stupid. I was no better than Chester Cole, pretending to myself I was superman. Hardy was a professional. Chambrun was a man with a degree in dealing with violence. The best I could hope for, to satisfy my need to get revenge for Shirley, was that they could use me somehow, that I could contribute.

"When you've been around as long as I have," Chambrun said, "you get so you can smell it." We were back in his office, and Hardy was on the phone to someone in the Hollywood police department. He wanted a check made on Claude Duval's whereabouts for the past twenty-four hours. With today's travel speeds a man could get a call on the West Coast in the early afternoon, fly to New York, and be back west again after midnight their time. There was no way Duval could have had a call from Shirley in the early afternoon and been here two hours later to shoot her and loot her apartment. The point was, had he ever been on the West Coast? Had Shirley got his answering machine in Hollywood and then found a way to reach him here? Chester Cole had suggested that not everyone who was supposed to have headed west had really gone.

What Chambrun said he could smell was fear. "When a man is as obviously frightened as Cole is," he said, "there's no use beating on him. Sooner or later he may get his nerve back, or he'll get so terrified he has to ask for help. I could see you wanted me to keep at him, Mark. Experience told me that now wasn't the moment."

Hardy came back from the phone to join us. "If Duval has been in Hollywood all day yesterday and today, we should know in a very few minutes," he said. "If he was filming, there'll be dozens of witnesses. If he was there, we can write him off."

Chambrun's eyes narrowed against the smoke from his cigarette. "We had a theory, Walter, early on, that someone had hired a professional to get into my apartment, open my safe, and carry me off to New Jersey. That professional carried the same kind of weapon as was used to murder Shirley Thomas. His employer didn't have to be anywhere near here. Alibis for that 'employer,' whoever he may be, don't mean a thing."

"You suspect Duval?" Hardy asked.

"So far he's just a name on a list as long as both our arms," Chambrun said. "So far as I know he isn't on any list you have of people who've been involved with Laura Kauffman. He didn't know her, according to Cole."

"'According to Cole' doesn't impress me," Hardy said. "That jerk was running for his life."

"I know," Chambrun said. He leaned back in his desk chair, his eyes almost closed. "Let's play games, Walter. The man who shot Shirley Thomas had a .44, same as my abductor. So let's say he is the same man, involved in both happenings. I was carried off to keep me from seeing someone or something. Not Laura Kauffman's murderer, because I was here, I was circulating when that happened. It was someone or something that came on the scene after that butchering. Now, Shirley Thomas was on the trail of people who might have been connected with Laura Kauffman through most of a lifetime. Aware or not, she must have been headed in the right direction. She had to be stopped. Her records had to be destroyed in case there was something there that would tell us where she was headed. I think we have to assume, Walter, that all three things, two murders and my abduction, involve the same man or men."

"I'm willing to assume it," Hardy said. "What else is there?"

"What did Shirley know about Laura Kauffman, Mark? Had Laura appeared in her column?" Chambrun asked.

"I suppose she did," I said. "International hostess, big party giver, operator in big charity drives. She appeared in all the gossip columns."

"After Laura was killed, what did Shirley tell you about her?"

"What she told Hardy. She didn't believe Laura had been raped. She'd have said 'yes' to anyone."

"But she didn't have any list of names for us," Hardy said.

"That kind of scandal wasn't Shirley's dish," I said.

"But she set out yesterday to get that kind of list for you, Walter," Chambrun said.

"She had the contacts, if she wanted to tap them," I said. "Like the Peyron woman in Paris."

"The Peyron woman didn't have anything immediate to give her," Hardy said. "So she calls Claude Duval in Hollywood."

"With how many local calls in between?" Chambrun asked. "She hadn't heard Chester Cole's statement that Duval and Laura were strangers, had she, Mark?"

"For God sake, boss, she was dead at the time Chester was telling me that—late yesterday afternoon."

"So being a good reporter she just followed a natural lead," Chambrun said. "She had started, through the Peyron woman, to try to delve into Laura's past in Paris. Duval, a Frenchman, must have known the Paris swim in those days. I'd have asked him."

"But she didn't get to ask him," Hardy said. "She got the mechanical answering service."

Chambrun's eyes were closed again. "He says," he said.

"If we could only talk to Shirley, know who she called, what she was looking for," I said. "Poor darling, she couldn't have dreamed she was in any danger."

"She went to her apartment to start digging for me about one o'clock in the afternoon," Hardy said. "Bernice Braden found her dead only about three hours later. She must have struck a nerve somewhere very early on."

Chambrun glanced at me. "You know who her friends are, Mark. Who would she have called for the kind of information she wanted? Other columnists? If we knew the kind of questions she was asking—"

"She always used to say the last person you'd go to for a story was a rival columnist," I said. " 'Exclusive' is the name of the game. Friends—?" I shrugged.

I think Chambrun understood. I didn't really know who Shirley's friends were. Our relationship, over a six-month period, had been so personal, so private. We hadn't been concerned with anyone but ourselves. We hadn't been party goers. She had to cover nightclubs, theater openings, high society windings. I didn't go to any of those things with her. My job kept me anchored at the Beaumont until about three in the morning. We joined up after she'd done her job and I'd done mine. Sundays, our mutual day off, we might drive out into the country, or just stay shacked up in my apartment, enjoying each other. She often had jokes about people, but famous people, not friends. There was a curtain drawn over her life before me. No mention of any other men, and I never mentioned other women. I was in love forever.

"Who do you know in the French embassy here, Mark?" Chambrun asked.

I knew the PR men for most of the UN delegations and the foreign governments in town. "Henri Latrobe," I said.

"See if Shirley called anyone there to ask questions," Chambrun said. "She had Paris on her mind."

I located Latrobe at his apartment, after persuading some gal at the embassy to give me his number. His day began in the early afternoon like most people who cover the night life in town. He had heard about Shirley. He was properly shocked. She had not called him and he thought she might have if she wanted something in his world. They had exchanged information in the past. He would check, but he was reasonably certain that, with the story of Shirley's death public property since the day before, he'd have heard if she'd called anyone.

Dead end.

When I rejoined Chambrun and Hardy to report—I'd made the call from Ruysdale's office—I found Frank Lewis, the FBI man, with them. He was just back from New Jersey.

"The cottage belongs to people named Hudson," he told us. "They're in Europe for the summer. They advertised their cottage for rent and the agent got a call from someone named Smith, of all things, wanting it. That was eight days ago. The agent, a busy man, never saw this Smith. The rent was delivered by hand when he was out of the office. A messenger service he thinks. One thousand and fifty dollars in cash."

"For eight days?" I asked.

"For three months at three hundred and fifty a month," Lewis said. "It's a good rent for a weekend summer cottage."

"All he wanted it for was to keep me out of sight for a day and a half," Chambrun said.

"Seems like," Lewis said. "Nobody saw him then or since. Neighbors didn't know the place was rented until you found someone to drive you into Princeton."

"Nothing in the cottage itself?" Chambrun asked.

"A pot of drugged coffee. Our department lab is checking out on it. This 'Smith' didn't even bother to get rid of it. Two coffee mugs, both with what I suspect are your prints on them. Nothing else that doesn't seem to relate to the owners."

Chambrun studied the ash on his cigarette, as though the moment it would drop into the ashtray was fascinating. "Most interesting thing about all this," he said, "is that they planned having me as a guest well in advance of the moment. Whoever or whatever I wasn't to see was prepared for ahead of time."

"And worth three months rent to cover who or what," Hardy said.

The little red light winked on Chambrun's phone. The call was for Hardy from his Hollywood police friend. The Hollywood cop had solved Hardy's problem with one phone call. Duval had been in Hollywood since midmorning after the ball here in New York. He had worked all day yesterday and until late in the evening at the studio, filming. The Hollywood cops could do a more thorough check if Hardy wanted, but there was no way Duval could have been in New York in the last forty-eight hours.

"So we're trying to fit a square peg into a round hole," Hardy said when he hung up.

Chambrun gave him a strange little smile. "It's been done before, Walter," he said. "As a matter of fact, we've done it." He paused to light a fresh cigarette. "We only have Duval's word that he didn't talk to Shirley. He admitted there'd been a call, registered on his answering machine. He had to admit that because we knew she'd made the call to his number. The fact is, she may have talked to him, and asked him a question or suggested something to him that triggered him into action."

"You're saying he's our 'employer'?" Hardy asked.

"We're just playing games, aren't we, Walter? If he is our employer, then his next action becomes obvious. Shirley, whether she knew it or not, had made herself dangerous to him."

"How, for God sake?" I asked.

"By suggesting to him, perhaps through a question, that if she continued her line of inquiry he was in trouble. So the 'employer' calls the 'employee' who is in New York and can get to Shirley in almost no time at all. Her inquiry is ended before she can make even a few more telephone calls."

"And we can't prove any part of it," Hardy said. He sounded tired of games. "So we're back at square one."

"Humor me, Walter," Chambrun said. "I'd like to play this out as far as it takes me."

Hardy shook his head. "I've got a list of names I got from James Kauffman which is, like you said, as long as my arm. I've got to check out on them before they all die of old age. Have fun, maestro."

When we were alone, Chambrun turned to me. "If I wasn't supposed to see someone, someone I didn't see was Duval," he said. "That fits, doesn't it? We have a man who won't let pictures be taken of him. So I would like to see one."

"But if there aren't any—?"

"He made a public appearance at the ball, I believe," Chambrun said. "There were all kinds of photographers in the press gallery. It may have been understood that no pictures of him be released, but for that very reason I'd like to bet someone has one."

Knowing press people and photographers is part of my job. I tried to remember who I'd seen in the press gallery the night of the ball. That night I'd been dancing with Shirley. For a moment I had that sick feeling, remembering what she'd felt like in my arms, the scent of her gold-blond hair. I pulled myself together and recalled Charlie Price, who takes pictures for International.

I got lucky. Charlie was at his office. I asked him if he'd taken any pictures of Duval at the Cancer Fund Ball.

"That's a no-no, chum," Charlie said.

"That doesn't mean you didn't take any for your memory book."

"Why do you want one?"

"My boss wants to see what Duval looks like," I said. "He'd consider it a favor, and you might be able to use a favor from him someday."

"It can't be released, Mark, or used for advertising or publicity," Charlie said.

"Chambrun just wants to know what he looks like," I said. "I told him Telly Savalas, but that isn't good enough."

"Not so funny you should say that," Charlie said. "People stop him on the street, thinking he's Savalas. If people ask him for autographs he signs Savalas's name. Look, I'll give you a print, but your boss has got to play by the rules or it's my neck."

At a little after two in the afternoon I presented Chambrun with a picture of Duval. It wasn't a studio shot. He was standing on the platform at the end of the ballroom, tweed jacket, tinted glasses, a beret on his bald head.

"Made a nice little speech of thanks to everyone," I said.

Chambrun stared at the picture for a long time. I thought he was disappointed. I don't know what he expected to see, but what was there obviously didn't forward his game.

Ruysdale appeared at the office door. "It's Chester Cole on the phone for you, Mark."

Chambrun switched on the squawk box and I

picked up the phone. Someone was breathing hard, like in those horror movies on TV.

"Chester?" I said.

"Mark? For the love of God come up here—now!" he said.

"What's wrong?"

"Just hurry! And bring your cop friend with you if you can."

I put down the phone.

"It's caught up with him," Chambrun said. "His panic."

We hurried down the hall to the elevators and went up to the ninth floor. Like the first time, Cole didn't answer his doorbell or a knock. Chambrun sent me down the hall for the maid's passkey.

We let ourselves in. Cole wasn't waiting for us. It was one of our French rooms, and a delicate little Louis XIV straight-backed chair was overturned on the rug. Not broken, just tipped over. Cole wasn't anywhere. A cigarette was burning in an ashtray on the bureau. We'd missed him by only that much.

There are two ways off any floor in the Beaumont, the elevators and the fire stairs. There are four elevators that come to nine, all with operators at that time of day. One of them remembered bringing Cole up about fifteen minutes ago—just before he'd called me. None of the four operators had seen him leave.

By the time Security had been alerted by Chambrun, Chester Cole had time to go almost anywhere, up, down, or out on the fire stairs. Jerry Dodd took over and came up empty after about an hour. He reported to Chambrun in his office.

"Donovan on elevator number three took him up,"

Jerry told us. "Nobody took him down. Fifteen minutes after he went up, you were there. You think he left on his own, or someone made him leave?"

"Who knows," Chambrun said. "He was scared out of his wits."

"People came up to nine and left it," Jerry said. "I could dig up a partial list. But nobody left with Cole—on the elevators. Who are we looking for?"

"I wish I knew," Chambrun said. "In a nonsensical game I'm playing it could be someone connected with Clark Herman's film company. Man without a face as far as I'm concerned."

There was a long and tedious search after that, much like the one that had been set in motion for Chambrun. I won't try to describe it. It didn't turn up Chester Cole anywhere.

I remember Chambrun, sitting at his desk, bringing his fist down hard on the polished surface.

"We don't catch up with them and these people will go on and on and on!" he said. "I want to talk to Duval."

"He's in Hollywood, as you know. I can probably dig up a number for him."

"I don't want to talk to him on the phone. I want him here."

"Not much chance of that, I'd think," I said. "He isn't likely to accept an invitation from you. What could the cops charge him with, and how could they get him back from California?"

"There has to be a way," Chambrun said.

When Chambrun says there has to be a way there is a way, but only someone as devious as Chambrun can be could come up with it. The rest of that afternoon I

was involved with two projects; trying to find someone who may have seen Chester Cole leave the hotel
while at the same time trying to stay within reach of a
phone in case Chester might call again; and working
in my office with Bernice Braden, Shirley's badly
shaken secretary, calling people she suggested Shirley
might have been in touch with in her quest for information about Laura Kauffman. I came up empty in
all directions. There was just one thing that I could
offer for the pot. The phone company told me that
Shirley's call to Duval in Hollywood had lasted less
than two minutes. They had the charges on it. That
seemed to back up Duval's story that she had gotten
the answering machine. A conversation with him,
even an unfruitful conversation, must have lasted
longer than two minutes.

I took this one fragment of information to Chambrun's office about seven o'clock in the evening. I
didn't get to give it to him just then because he had
company. Sitting comfortably in one of the green
leather armchairs was Mrs. Victoria Haven, smoking a
cigarette in a long jade holder, and cradling that
nasty-looking little Japanese spaniel in her ample lap.
She had on a black evening dress, a summer fur
draped over her shoulders, and was decked out in
enough jewelry to sink a tugboat. She gave me an
amiable smile and Toto growled at me.

The other guest was Henri Latrobe from the French
embassy. Latrobe is a dark, handsome young man
about my age, with a perpetual smile and laughing
dark eyes. He was wearing a dinner jacket with black
pearl studs in a very mod, lace-frilled dress shirt. He
looked pleased with himself.

"You have arrived just in time to be in on a deception, Mark," Chambrun said.

"I should be clear to you, Mark," Henri Latrobe said, "that my mother should never know about this. She is a good Catholic."

Toto growled at me and Mrs. Haven said: "Do shut up, Toto." Then to me, "I have never objected to lying in a good cause, Mark."

I didn't know what the hell they were talking about. The red light blinked on Chambrun's phone. He switched on the squawk box and picked up.

"I have Mr. Duval for you, Mr. Chambrun," the operator said.

Chambrun nodded to Henri Latrobe. Latrobe winked at me and said: "Claude? Henri Latrobe here. I'm afraid I have some trouble for you."

"Something wrong with my passport?" Duval asked. He sounded undisturbed. "I'm in the middle of shooting an important sequence, Henri." I realized it would be about four in the afternoon on the coast.

"Nothing like that," Henri said. "It's trouble with the film, though."

"What kind of trouble?" Duval asked.

"There is an elderly lady who lives here at the Hotel Beaumont," Henri said.

"What elderly lady?"

"A Mrs. Victoria Haven."

"I never heard of her," Duval said.

"I'm afraid you will, Claude," Henri said. "The lady is about to make big trouble for you."

"How would you like to come to the point?" Duval asked in a flat, cold voice. His British accent made it sound clipped.

"It has to do with the filming here at the Cancer Fund Ball, and later in the Trapeze Bar," Henri said. "Mrs. Haven was present on both occasions."

I looked at the old girl, who was smiling happily. I remembered distinctly her telling us she hadn't been at the ball, and I could swear she hadn't been in the Trapeze. Shirley and I had been there when the film was being shot with Janet Parker and Robert Randle.

"So she was present," Duval said. "What of it?"

"She is getting an injunction from a friendly judge to prevent your using any of that footage, Claude. She's in both sets of film and she will not allow you to use them without her personal permission. Invasion of privacy. I think she's got you over a barrel, Claude."

"So get her permission," Duval said. "There are hundreds of thousands of dollars involved."

"Mrs. Haven is here with me," Henri said. "Perhaps you can persuade her."

"Put her on," Duval said.

Mrs. Haven cleared her throat and spoke in her husky, whiskey voice. "I don't want to discuss matters on the telephone, Mr. Duval," she said.

"I will have the producer's lawyer call on you in the morning, madam."

"I will only talk to you, and in person," Victoria Haven said.

"That's quite out of the question," Duval said. "I am in the middle of a filming here."

"Then you will be served with an injunction in the morning," Mrs. Haven said. "Goodnight, Mr. Duval."

"Latrobe!" Duval shouted.

"Yes, Claude." Henri was grinning like a cat.

"Can't you talk some sense into that woman?"

"I think you're the only one, Claude. Before I called I looked up plane schedules. There's a flight leaving Los Angeles International in about fifty minutes. Gets you into Kennedy about one o'clock. You could just about make it."

"One o'clock!" Duval said. "Eight hours! What kind of flight is that?"

"Difference in time, Claude. Five-hour flight."

"Will that old bitch see me at that time of night?"

"That old bitch, Mr. Duval, is a night person," Victoria Haven said.

"I'm sorry, madam. I didn't realize—"

"Realize that this is no laughing matter, Mr. Duval," she said.

"I wouldn't waste time, Claude," Henri said. "I'll call the airport and arrange a seat for you. Diplomatic pressure. With the time difference you can be back at your studio first thing in the morning."

"The whole thing is pure idiocy," Duval said. "But— I'll make the five o'clock flight."

The phone went dead.

Chambrun gave Latrobe a thin smile. "You were first rate, Henri," he said.

"I take particular pleasure in making trouble for that genius," Henri said. "He's been demanding outrageous favors from my government for twenty years— ever since he became The Great One in motion pictures."

"If he stops to look at the rushes of the film they shot here," Mrs. Haven said, "he'll know that I am lying in my teeth. I'm obviously not in any of the film they shot because I wasn't in either place."

"He can look at the rushes until he's cross-eyed," Chambrun said. "He won't know whether you're in them or not because he doesn't know what you look like."

"How lucky for him," the old lady said, with a touch of bitterness.

"My dear Victoria, I find you beautiful and irresistible," Chambrun said.

"I, too, find you that," Henri said. He reached out to take her hand, a kissing of the fingers in the offing. Toto snarled at him.

Chambrun leaned back in his desk chair, still smiling. "So we have about six hours to wait," he said.

"He didn't seem to resist the idea of coming here," I said. "Maybe he doesn't care whether you see him or not."

"I think he won't expect me to be here," Chambrun said.

I didn't realize until later exactly what he meant by that.

THREE

Maybe I didn't want to know what he meant. But about ten thirty he made it quite clear to others as well as me. Ruysdale, Jerry Dodd, and Hardy were gathered with him when I answered a summons that reached me out in the "circulating area."

Chambrun, dinner jacketed, was sitting at his desk when I arrived, sipping at a glass of white wine poured over shaved ice, his usual evening drink. He didn't look relaxed, though. His eyes were very bright, and he kept turning the wine glass round and round in his fingers.

"The whole thing is based on pure fantasy, made out of something lighter than air," he said. "It begins on a supposition based on almost nothing. I was abducted from my penthouse, apparently to keep me from seeing someone. It happens that I never saw Claude Duval."

"Or several hundred other people," Hardy said, "whom you can't even name."

"Humor me, Walter," Chambrun said. "Poor Shirley Thomas is asking questions about Laura Kauffman. She's asking those questions on the telephone from her apartment. She isn't facing anyone with awkward questions, yet somebody comes to her apartment and puts an end to it. It so happens one of the people she talked to was Claude Duval."

"She talked to a mechanical answering service," Hardy said.

"Duval says. In my fantasy she talked to him. Now, we have considered the likelihood of an 'employer' with a hired professional strong-arm man who is also an expert at locks. Shirley asks a dangerous question and Duval, who is the 'employer' in my dream, gets in touch with his professional who is here in New York, and half an hour later Shirley is dead."

"If I were to act on this kind of fantasy," Hardy said, "they'd have my gun and badge and I'd be locked up in a state mental hospital for observation."

"But I don't have a gun or a badge to lose, Walter," Chambrun said, "and I'm not responsible to anyone but myself for my dreams."

"So dream on," Hardy said.

"Chester Cole told Mark that Duval didn't know Laura Kauffman. Laura went to his suite to talk about the ball, Cole was there, and he's certain they didn't know each other. I permit myself the luxury of dreaming that they *did* know each other. She was living in Paris in the black days of the Nazi occupation. He is a Frenchman and is old enough to have been living then. In my fantasy, they knew each other but didn't reveal the fact in Cole's presence. Later Laura gets in touch with Duval, or he gets in touch with her. He goes to see her. She is a blackmailer and she tries it on for size. Either Duval blows his stack and puts an end to her himself, or he goes away and sends for his professional hit-man to do the job for him."

"Invent me a piece of evidence, chum, out of your whole cloth," Hardy said.

"Patience, Walter, I'm about to do just that. It is all fantasy, all nonsense—or it can be true," Chambrun said. "If it is true, there are certain things we can expect. Duval, we know, is due to arrive at Kennedy at one o'clock. He should reach the Beaumont not later than one thirty. If my dream, to mix a metaphor, will hold water, and it was dangerous for me to see him when he was here for the ball, then it would still be dangerous."

"In your dream, why are you so goddamned dangerous to him?" Hardy asked. He was irritated, almost angry with his friend.

"I haven't the faintest idea, Walter," Chambrun said, smiling. "But he risked the possibility of having to murder me, risked a kidnapping charge to remove me from the hotel. That makes me really dangerous."

"It's still pure fantasy that Duval is your 'employer.'"

"I like the word 'pure,'" Chambrun said. "No proof, but I believe it for the moment. I intend to try to prove it before he gets here."

"How?"

"By going to bed early," Chambrun said, and sipped his wine.

"Oh, for God sake, Pierre!" Hardy said. "Stop wasting our time."

Chambrun lit one of his flat Egyptian cigarettes. "If it was so dangerous for me to see Duval two days ago it is still equally dangerous. So I will make a public point of going to bed early. If I am right, I will have a visitor sometime before Duval arrives."

"A visitor?"

"A man who understands locks and who carries a .44 handgun," Chambrun said.

"You think that creep will pay you a second visit?" Jerry Dodd asked.

"If any of this fantasy is for real," Chambrun said, "I think he will. At the best—for me, that is—I must be occupied when Duval visits the hotel. At the worst—for me—I had better be dead, out of the way permanently. Whatever the decision, I think he will almost certainly try to get to me. So, I will 'go to bed early,' try to make it easy for him."

"Make it easy?" Jerry asked.

"He got into the penthouse once. He knows how," Chambrun said. "The difference this time is that I'll be expecting him."

"I should have my head examined," Hardy said, "but we'll all be waiting for him. But why not here, Pierre? We can protect you a great deal better here; cover the elevators, the corridor outside, Miss Ruysdale's office."

"Does it occur to you, Walter, that if I am obviously protected he may, in desperation, take a long shot at me from somewhere. That's too hard to guard against. I want to make it easy for him. I don't want him to dream for a moment that I expect him."

"So he lets himself into the penthouse and blasts away at you with his .44," Hardy said.

"I think not," Chambrun said. "I think not while I am warned and ready."

"How can we warn you?" I asked. "We can cover every entrance to the hotel and not know when he walks in. We don't know what he looks like! He won't come charging into the lobby wearing his ski mask!"

I should have known he had it carefully planned. He would go to the penthouse. He would begin to play music on his stereo, as he always did. The elevators to the roof and the roof itself would be left unguarded. Hardy, and whatever extra men he wanted, would be waiting on the floor below the roof level.

"But I will be warned when he reaches the roof level," Chambrun said.

"How?"

Chambrun gave us a delighted grin. "By a little dog who will bark his head off at any intruder," Chambrun said. "Victoria Haven has agreed to let Toto loose on the roof the moment I'm in the penthouse. That little bastard will be better than a burglar alarm as soon as a stranger enters his domain."

"You're kidding!" Hardy said.

"Toto will be as predictable and precise as an electric eye," Chambrun said. "His whole life is devoted to protecting Victoria from strangers—even friends. He will warn me, and I will be waiting just inside the penthouse door for my visitor."

"The only reason I buy it," Hardy said, "is that the whole thing simply isn't going to happen."

"There is one other very important part to my plan," Chambrun said. "I think it falls to you, Jerry. I want the plane from Los Angeles to be met at Kennedy. You'll have no difficulty spotting this Telly Savalas type getting off the plane. I think the first thing he will do is head for a telephone."

"Why?" Jerry asked.

"He will be calling his man, his professional, his killer, to make sure his mission is accomplished. I am dead, I am silenced, I will not be here at the Beaumont to confront him. But if we have been successful on this end, Duval won't be able to reach his man. What he does then is important for us to know. Will he risk coming here anyway? Will he take flight? Will he

try to arrange with Mrs. Haven to meet her somewhere else? We mustn't lose him, Jerry."

"That's a job for cops. I want to stay here by you,"
Jerry said.

"I appreciate that, friend," Chambrun said. "But
cops look like cops. I don't want to scare him off."

"But he may recognize me," Jerry said. "I was on
stage, you might say, during the ball."

"Then you just walk up to him and say the hotel
sent you to make sure he had no problems getting to
Mrs. Haven. You'll have your own car. A special cour-
tesy, arranged by Mrs. Haven." Chambrun's smile was
wry. "The Beaumont is famous for special courtesies."

I found out then what my part in this charade was
to be. I was to spend the rest of the evening with Mrs.
Haven in her penthouse.

"She is an extraordinary woman, Mark," Chambrun
said. "She is also a very loyal friend. If she thought
something was going wrong, she might try to get into
the act. You're to see to it that she doesn't. Just stay
with her, see that she lets Toto out onto the roof, and
nothing else. When Toto warns us, as I believe he will,
just stay put and see to it that Victoria stays put."

Jerry grinned at me. "You think you can handle an
eighty-year-old doll?" he asked.

"I'm not at all sure," I said.

"You and your men, Walter, will be in a suite on the
floor below," Chambrun said. "Mark will alert you the
minute Toto warns us. You will stay there, however, until he warns you a second time."

"A second time?" I asked.

"If all of the lights don't go on in my penthouse
within ten minutes of Toto's alarm, it will probably
mean that I've failed," Chambrun said. "If they do go

on, it means I've got him. Either way it will be time for the marines."

At about eleven thirty Mrs. Haven greeted me at the door of her penthouse. She was wearing a wine-red, tentlike housecoat, a drink in one hand and her long jade cigarette holder in the other. Toto growled at me from his satin cushion.

"A pretty dull prospect for you, Mark," she said. "Spending the evening with the ancient wreck of a woman. I can remember—well, never mind what I can remember. Drink?"

I thought a bourbon on the rocks would be a nice idea.

She weaved her way through the piles of junk in her living room to a little portable bar in a far corner and made me my drink.

"Thank goodness it's not raining," she said. "If it was raining, Toto would be no use."

"Oh?"

"He'll prowl around on the roof forever," she said. "But if it rains, he'll be clawing at the door, paying no attention to anything but getting in."

"There's a bright moon and stars," I said.

"Do we let him out now?" she asked.

I walked over to the window facing Chambrun's penthouse and pulled aside the heavy drapes enough to peek out. Just then dim lights popped on across the way. Chambrun was there.

"I guess it's now," I said.

Mrs. Haven picked up the little dog from his satin cushion and kissed him right on his pug nose. "Now you go out, darling," she said. "Have fun, and keep away any naughty people."

A bright red tongue licked her wrinkled cheek. She carried him to the door and let him out.

"Now we wait," Mrs. Haven said. "How long, do you think?"

"Who knows?" I said.

Her pale old eyes were narrowed with concern. "Pierre is too old to be playing games like this," she said. "I should have refused him, only he would have gone on just the same without my help."

"He's not an easy man to say 'no' to," I said. "As for being too old, he's in his fifties. Prime of life, he calls it."

"He is fifty-eight, by my reckoning," she said. "I first knew him thirty-five years ago during what he calls 'the black days' in Paris. He was a wild young man with the heart of a lion back then. He was better up to confronting psychotic killers in those days. But now?" She looked down at her wrinkled hand and suddenly put it out of sight in the pocket of her robe. "The body doesn't respond to the impulses of the mind after a while, Mark."

"But the mind can outthink the opposition—I hope," I said.

"The place is swarming with police. Why doesn't he leave it to them?"

"We don't know who we're looking for," I said. "We have to bait a trap for him."

"With Pierre as bait?" she asked. "I don't like it, Mark."

"Like I said, he's a hard man to say 'no' to."

Smoke swirled around her hennaed hair from the cigarette in her holder. She was looking away from me, toward the past, I thought.

"I once said 'no' to him, and lived to regret it." She

turned her head and caught me smiling. "Oh, not what you think, Mark. There's no way, by any magic, to make me anything less than twenty-five years older than Pierre—at any time that I've known him. He was twenty-three when I first met him, I was forty-eight. Had he not been so young he might have guessed that at forty-eight I could have been a pretty sensational sex partner. I think I was at *my* best then. And, he was too busy destroying and killing Nazis. He didn't need what I had to offer then to prove his manhood. In a life that has known romance I have regretted that." She sighed. "But later he offered me friendship, and that I cherish. That's why I'm sitting here with you waiting for Toto to tell us something."

"But you said 'no' to him about something else?"

Talk was the best way to pass time. From the moment Victoria Haven had put that nasty little spaniel out onto the roof I'd felt tensions growing in me unitl they were almost unbearable. I listened to this nice old woman, going on in her hoarse, whiskey voice, but most of all I listened for some sound of protest from Toto. I glanced at my watch every two or three minutes. It was almost midnight. If the "professional" was coming ahead of Duval, it would have to be relatively soon.

"He asked me, once, a long time ago, to help a man who was in desperate trouble," Mrs. Haven said, looking back again. "I am very well off, Mark. I've always been lucky enough to have a great deal of money. Pierre, at the time, had just begun his career here at the Beaumont and he had no more than a modestly good salary. I said 'no' because I didn't like the man he wanted me to help. I didn't like him because he was German, and we had just suffered too much from Germans in those days."

I was only half listening. Would I hear that bloody little dog when he barked? If he barked!

"You can imagine this is all very vivid to me right now," Mrs. Haven said, "when I tell you that the man was the Baron von Holtzmann, Laura Kauffman's husband at the time. You may know that he committed suicide. If I had been willing to help—who knows?"

That jolted me. "You knew her back then? You knew him?"

She nodded. "I had no use for her. She was a collaborator with the Nazis. In my book, Mark, she got what she deserved here the other night. Von Holtzmann was just another German to me. Pierre told me he had actually been fighting the Nazis, helping the Resistance. I chose not to put much stock in that. He was German! Like most of Laura's men he lived off her money. Hemmerly steel. When he left her, for whatever reason, he was without funds and I gather deeply in debt. He borrowed from what Pierre described as loan sharks. He had to pay, or else. He chose his own way out. I was sorry, then, that I'd refused Pierre. I should have trusted his judgment. I always have since then. That's why—"

She didn't finish. From out on the roof came the high, shrill barking of the little spaniel.

I had my instructions. I reached for the phone. Miss Kiley, on the switchboard, was waiting for my signal.

"Hardy," I said to her.

Seconds later Hardy answered.

"The dog," I said to him.

"I have fourteen minutes past twelve," Hardy said. "In ten minutes I come up whether you call or not. See anything?"

"Chambrun told me not to part the drapes, not to show a light from here," I said. "In ten minutes—"

Mrs. Haven was on her feet, a hand resting on my shoulder. She was trembling. I held out my left arm and we both watched the second hand on my watch drag its way around the dial. A minute, two minutes, three minutes.

"I can't stand this," the old woman said. "Let's go to him." She picked up a handbag from the table and, to my surprise, produced a small, pearl-handled revolver.

"I gave my word we'd both stay put for a full ten minutes," I said.

The dog was still barking, angrily. I think we both expected the next thing we'd hear was the sound of a gunshot. At twenty-one minutes past twelve I opened the drapes a slit. All the lights were on in Chambrun's penthouse.

I grabbed up the phone again and told Hardy. Then I ran out onto the roof. The little spaniel made a grab at my trouser leg as I ran past him at the door. I sensed that Mrs. Haven was behind me, moving as fast as her ancient legs would carry her.

The door to Chambrun's place was open, lights blazing inside. I charged through the little foyer and nearly fell flat on my face as I stumbled over an inert figure stretched out on the floor. For an awful moment I thought it was Chambrun. Then, as I regained my balance, I saw him. There are two steps leading down from the foyer into the living room. He was sitting on the top step, just to the left of the body, holding the poker from his set of fire irons.

"I think I've killed him," he said in a flat, faraway voice.

I looked down at the man on the floor. There was an ugly, bleeding wound at the side of his head. The room was filled with the climactic music from Beethoven's Fifth Symphony. There was something familiar about the wounded man, and I bent down to get a better look at his face which was buried in the rug.

He was the anonymous little man I had assumed to be Duval's secretary.

The room was suddenly flooded with people; Hardy and three plainclothes cops, Betsy Ruysdale, who'd evidently been with Hardy, waiting, and Mrs. Haven, holding the snarling little spaniel in her arms. Our hero!

I remember Ruysdale turning off the stereo and going to sit by Chambrun. Hardy was kneeling by the secretary's body—had they said his name was Jacques Bordeau?—feeling for a throat pulse. He looked up and the expression on his face gave us an answer. Bordeau was not going to tell us anything, now or ever!

"When the dog barked—and bless him, Victoria," Chambrun said, "I took up a position just inside the front door—with this." He held out the poker. "I thought I would simply knock the gun out of his hand if he had one. I had the music going. He knew how to work the lock. He pushed the door in, but he was turned at such an angle that we were instantly facing each other. That .44—I think it's under him—was aimed straight at my gut. There was no time to be clever. I just brought the poker down on his head with all the strength I have. He was so shocked to find me there, facing him, that his reactions failed him. He lost a heartbeat in time, and in losing it, lost his only chance." He glanced at his watch. "We don't have time to get to the airport to intercept Duval," he said "We'll have to trust Jerry."

"I can reach police at the airport," Hardy said. "We have reason to arrest him now if this is his man."

"It's his man," I said.

The scene at the airport must have been tense, if brief. According to Jerry Dodd, Duval came off the plane and, exactly as Chambrun had predicted, headed for a pay telephone. He dialed a number, waited; dialed it again and waited. He came out of the booth angry and anxious, and found himself confronted by Jerry.

"I'm from the hotel, Mr. Duval," Jerry said. "I've brought a car. Taxis are sometimes hard to come by at this time in the morning."

"I'm not going directly to the Beaumont," Duval told him. "Thanks all the same."

He started to move away and found two plain-clothes cops standing on either side of him.

"Your secretary has been killed at the Hotel Beaumont," he was told. "You are wanted there for questioning."

Jerry told us that Duval's expression didn't alter by a hair; no shock, no surprise. It was as though he was prepared.

"So be it," was all he said.

It was about a quarter past two in the morning when the two plainclothes men and Jerry delivered Duval to Chambrun's office at the hotel. Chambrun was sitting at his desk. I was there along with Hardy and Betsy Ruysdale.

It was a strange moment. Chambrun's hooded eyes were fixed intently on Duval. Duval, his shaved head gleaming in the light from the chandelier, seemed unaware of anyone else but Chambrun. Finally it was Chambrun who spoke.

"You've had some rather elaborate cosmetic surgery done, Perrault," he said.

Perrault! The name came up into focus. Hugo Perrault, known thirty-five years ago as the mad Butcher of Montmartre. Dead more than thirty years, if I remembered Chambrun's story correctly. A plane crash while trying to escape from Paris; the man from whom Chambrun had escaped in Laura Hemmerly's apartment in Paris during the occupation.

"When a man has faced death, no amount of disguise will hide his would-be killer," Duval said, quietly. "The eyes. There is no way to disguise the eyes." He drew a deep breath. "I wonder if I might have a glass of water?"

Ruysdale moved to Chambrun's desk and poured water into a glass from a thermos jug there. She took it to Duval.

"Thank you," Duval said. "I have a splitting headache." He took a flat tin of aspirin tablets from his pocket and quickly swallowed a couple of them.

Chambrun half rose from his chair, and then settled back, his face a rock-hard mask.

"They've told you about Bordeau," Hardy said. "Mr. Chambrun killed him before he could kill Mr. Chambrun."

"You still are able to move quickly, Chambrun," Duval said. "I must move quickly now."

"I know," Chambrun said.

"Jacques Bordeau was the son of a close associate of

mine in the days when I first knew you, Chambrun,"
Duval said. "A terrorist of the first order, finally
wanted by police all over Europe. I took him under
my wing because I thought, some day, he might be
useful. Violence was all that gave him pleasure. It was
to him what heroin is to an addict. When I had to
come here for the filming, I knew I couldn't risk your
identifying me."

"What could Chambrun do if he identified you?"
Hardy asked.

"You don't understand the world of the past, Lieutenant," Duval said. "There are underground forces,
mainly in Israel, still searching for what they call war
criminals. Men like Eichmann, men like me. They
think of us as Jew killers. Identified, I would be
snatched away, tried, executed.

"That plane crash, thirty-three years ago, I did not
die in it as you can see, Chambrun. But I was terribly
burned. A plastic surgeon built me a new face. I had a
chance to make a new life. I did. I took a new name. I
have reached the top of my profession as a director of
films. Only once or twice in all that time has there
been a danger of exposure. I knew, when it was
decided to film here at the Beaumont, that there was
the risk of your spotting me, Chambrun. Bordeau and
I arranged to have you absent. You were not to be
harmed unless you made it necessary. You didn't make
it necessary."

"But you found you had another enemy in the hotel," Chambrun said.

The corner of Duval's mouth twitched. "Laura
Hemmerly," he said, "now Mrs. Kauffman. I didn't
dream who she was—this Mrs. Kauffman—when I sent

for her to discuss the filming schedule with her. When she came into my suite I couldn't believe it. Thirty-five years ago I had been her lover in Paris. That was why she set you up that time in the Avenue Klebert, Chambrun. I was her man. But—when that plane crashed and I was, as you might say, rebuilt, no one could know, not even a lover. So, three days ago I found myself facing her. I knew who she was, but I wasn't sure she'd recognized me—till she phoned. She knew, and she would use what she knew. I knew I was in the clutches of a blackmailer forever. So—I turned Bordeau loose. I think he took a spectacular pleasure in what he did."

"Bastard!" Jerry Dodd said.

"As I said, violence was Jacques's special delight."

"I think I must hurry you, Duval," Chambrun said. "Why Shirley Thomas?"

"An unfortunate situation," Duval said. "I regret it, though I suspect that doesn't matter to you. She called me."

"And got the answering machine?"

"I'm afraid I didn't quite tell your Los Angeles policeman the truth. She got me. She told me she was helping the police dig out facts about Laura Kauffman. She had a list of names, given her by Laura's husband. Laura had evidently taunted him with her past adventures. Near the head of the list was one Hugo Perrault. Did I know anything about him—since I must have lived in Paris at that time?" Duval shook his head. "Was she on to me? Was that why she asked me? I couldn't risk it. I told her I couldn't discuss it then but would she be at home at three thirty. I would call her then. Of course I had no intention of

calling her. I just wanted to be sure she'd be at home
when Bordeau went to see her. I called him, gave him
his orders."

"You sonofabitch!" I heard myself say.

"About Chester Cole," Chambrun asked. "What has
happened to him?"

"Cole is—is somewhere at the far ends of the earth,"
Duval said. "He—he had dug up something about Bordeau's past, not mine. He was on the point of telling
you, Bordeau thought. Bordeau frightened Cole out of
his life and he took off for God knows where."

Duval lifted a hand to his throat and made a little
moaning sound. "When Cole hears—that we are both
dead—he will reappear."

Duval dropped down on his hands and knees and
then rolled over on his back and lay there, gasping for
breath. Hardy rushed to him.

"Nothing you can do, Walter," Chambrun said. "In
the old days, the days of the first terror, men like Duval, men like me, carried with us the way out. You
will find those aren't aspirin tablets in that little tin
box."

"You let him do it?" Hardy said.

Chambrun's hands were quite steady as he lit a cigarette. "It will save us being involved in a long, sensational trial. Does it matter who stopped him, the law
or himself?"

He didn't say it, but I can imagine he was thinking
he had a hotel to run and nothing must interfere with
that.